# THE TEFLON QUEEN

A NOVEL BY

SILK WHITE

GOOD2GO PUBLISHING

# SILK WHITE

Published by:
GOOD2GO PUBLISHING
7311 W. Glass Lane
Laveen, AZ 85339
www.good2gopublishing.com
www.silkwhite.com
facebook/silkwhite
twitter @good2gobooks
silkwhite212@yahoo.com
G2G@good2gopublishing.com

ThirdLane Marketing: Brian James
Brian@good2gopublishing.com

Cover design: Davida Baldwin
Edited by: Kesha Buckhana
Typesetter: Rukyyah
ISBN: 978-0-615-54952-1

# PROLOGUE

Jerry Bourne sat in the back of his limousine sipping on a glass of wine, enjoying the nice cool breeze from the air conditioner. In between his legs, sat a metal briefcase. Jerry didn't know what was inside the briefcase, all he knew was his boss was paying him a ton of money just for him to deliver it to a few Mexican men over at the Ramada Hotel.

On any other given day, Jerry would have never been caught dead in a place like that, but today was different. Today Jerry was more than happy to step foot in the Ramada, especially since he was getting paid for the job.

Once the limo pulled up in front of the hotel, Jerry quickly hopped out and power walked inside the building. He held on to the briefcase like it was a newborn baby as he walked pass the middle class people heading towards the room he was told to meet the Mexican men. Jerry hated poor people, and he hated being anywhere around them. He couldn't wait to make the drop off so he could hurry up and be back on his way out of Slumville as he called it.

When Jerry reached the room he was looking for, he took a deep breath and knocked lightly on the door. Seconds later, a Mexican man with a thick mustache answered the door with a no nonsense look on his face.

"Come in!" he ordered, moving to the side so Jerry could enter the room.

Jerry stepped in the room and immediately was scared to death when he saw four rough looking, Mexican men with bodies full of tattoos standing up all holding automatic weapons.

"How you doing guys?" Jerry asked in a friendly tone.

# THE TEFLON QUEEN

"What's in the case?" One of the Mexican men asked never taking his eyes off of Jerry. The Mexican's could smell fear coming off of Jerry as he stood there with a stupid look on his face.

"I don't know," Jerry said nervously. "My orders were to just drop the case off to you guys and then I'd be on my way," he said handing the briefcase to one of the Mexican's. Jerry turned and got ready to leave until a strong hand grabbed his shoulder stopping him in mid-stride.

"Leaving already?" One of the Mexican's asked.

"Yeah; I really need to get going... I have to go pick my wife up from work," Jerry lied.

"I think you might want to hang around," the leader of the group said. "At least until we make sure everything that's supposed to be in the case is in here."

"Sure, no problem," Jerry agreed. The longer he stood in the hotel room with the Mexican men, the more his body began to sweat.

"Why you look so nervous?" the leader asked.

"I'm fine," Jerry replied. "Just hurry up so I can be on my way."

The leader of the group smiled as he popped up the locks on the briefcase. Just as he got ready to open the briefcase, a silenced 9mm bullet pierced through his skull dropping him right where he stood; spilling blood and brain fragments on the rest of his crew.

The other three Mexican men looked around at each other wondering what had just happened. Blood was everywhere and the three men didn't even hear a gun shot. Immediately, all three men turned their attention on Jerry.

# SILK WHITE

"You set us up!" One of the Mexican men yelled as he raised his automatic weapon and aimed it at Jerry's head.

Jerry shut his eyes and braced himself for the bullet that would take his life, silencing him forever. After fifteen seconds had passed, Jerry finally decided to open his eyes. When Jerry looked up, he saw blood everywhere along with all four of the Mexican men laid out on the floor. Each man had a bullet hole directly in the middle of their foreheads.

"Shit!" Jerry cursed, wondering if he himself had been setup or used for bait. As Jerry stood there, his mind began wondering what was in the briefcase. He quickly locked the briefcase back up, snatched it off the bed, and exited the murder scene. Jerry took hurried steps until he finally reached the front of the hotel. Jerry breathed a sigh of relief when he saw his limousine waiting for him curbside.

"Get me as far away from here as possible!" Jerry huffed, happy to finally be out of harm's way.

As he got ready to open up the briefcase, he noticed that his driver hadn't pulled off yet. "Hey! I said get me the fuck out of here!" he repeated. "Hey Ben! Do you hear me talking to you? I said get me out of here!"

When the glass that separated Jerry and the driver rolled down, Jerry couldn't believe his eyes. Instead of Ben, a beautiful woman with long, beautiful, silky hair sat behind the wheel. "Hey Jerry," Angela said with a smile.

Jerry had never seen her before, but when he looked in her eyes, he knew exactly who he was looking in the eyes of… Angela who was also known as the Teflon Queen.

POW! She put a bullet right between his eyes, snatched the briefcase from off of his lap, and pulled off as if nothing ever happened.

# CHAPTER 1

Capo pulled his Benz up to the curb and placed the car in park. He was highly upset that he had to come out of his house just to handle some business for his boss Wayne. In the passenger seat sat Capo's main man, Moose, who had just come home from doing a long prison bid. "How much this nigga Max owe again?" Capo asked reading a text message from off of his iPhone.

"$15,000.00" Moose replied. "The nigga ain't call or been answering his jack," he added.

"Fuck it! Let's do it," Capo said as he hopped out the Benz with a bottle of Rosay in his hand. As the two men made their way inside the building, the few men who stood out in front of the building greeted them as if they were celebrities. Moose gave each man dap, while Capo just gave them a head nod and kept it moving. Capo was a straight up loose cannon. He loved to show off and be the center of attention, but his main thing was the ladies. Capo was a ladies man and planned on sleeping with as many women as he could either before he died or went to jail. Some people liked him, but most people really feared him and just pretended to like him so they could stay cool with him. Capo was light skin, stood about 6 feet tall, and favored the rapper Cam'ron.

"Yo come on," Capo huffed. "What you giving all them niggaz dap for?" He asked shaking his head as the two men hopped on the elevator.

Inside the apartment, Max sat on the couch with his girlfriend Shekia watching B.E.T while her mother cooked dinner. Max knew he was in deep shit. He just prayed he had a few more days to come up with the money. He knew Wayne didn't play when it came to his money. Max cursed himself repeatedly for losing most of the $15,000.00 in a dice game. He didn't mean any harm. He was just trying to flip his money. He had been staying over at his girlfriend Shekia's house, calling himself laying low.

"I'll be right back," Shekia said as she got up and headed to the bathroom.

"This the apartment right here?" Capo asked as he pulled out his .45.

"Yeah," Moose replied pulling out his twin 9's. Capo aimed his gun at the lock and pulled the trigger. Once the shot was fired, Moose quickly came forward and kicked open the door as the two rushed in the apartment.

"Yo, what the fuck is going on?" Max yelled with a scared look on his face.

"Shut the fuck up!" Moose growled as he backslapped Max with one of his 9's.

"Get out of my house or I'm going to call the police!" Shekia's mother yelled as she entered the living room. Before she could say another word, Capo busted her over the head with the Rosay bottle and watched her crumble down to the floor. Capo placed his foot on the woman's throat as he aimed the gun at her head. "Where's the money?" he asked talking to Max but still looking at the helpless woman he stood over.

"All I need is another week," Max said as if he was good for it. Capo lifted his arm and sent a shot in Max's direction. POW! The shot ripped through Max's shoulder forcing him to flop down on the couch.

"Wayne wants his money today! Do you have it or not?" Capo asked running out of patience.

# SILK WHITE

Shekia stood in the bathroom drying her hands when she heard what sounded like a gunshot. *"What the hell?"* She thought out loud, as she rushed out the bathroom and into the living room. Immediately, Moose trained his twin 9's on the woman. "Bitch get down on the floor now!" he barked. Not being a fool Shekia quickly did as she was told.

"Last time," Capo said. "Do you have the money or not?" Before Max even got a chance to answer, Capo had already fired off two shots killing him instantly. Once his body hit the floor, Moose walked over, stood over Max's body, and sent six more bullets into his body. Capo then walked over to Shekia who was now begging for her life.

"No please," Shekia begged. "My mother and I have nothing to do with this."

"Is this trash your boyfriend?" Capo asked sending one last shot into Max's lifeless body. Shekia didn't speak she just nodded her head yes.

"Well he owes my boss money so if you or your mother don't have $15,000.00 then there's nothing I can do for y'all."

"Wait!" Shekia said. "How about if I work off the debt," she suggested. She knew it was a long shot, but there was no way she was just going to sit there and watch her mother get killed.

Capo looked over at Moose. "What you think?"

"I say we kill both of these bitches and get up outta here," Moose answered honestly. Capo looked over at the woman and felt sorry for her. "Tell you what," Capo said placing his gun back in his waistband. "Here's my number. Call me in 48 hours and you better be ready to work!" he told her as he scribbled his number down on a piece of paper and handed it to her. "And baby girl," he said looking in Shekia's eyes. "Please don't try and contact the police. If you do, I promise you will regret it," Capo said with a smirk as he and Moose exited the apartment leaving Shekia with a decision to make. Capo just hoped she chose the right one.

"I don't know why you didn't just kill that bitch," Moose said when the two made it downstairs. "What if she goes to the cops?"

"Relax," Capo said nonchalantly. "Half the cops in New York city are on Wayne's pay roll. You worry too much." Capo shook his head as he hopped back in his Benz and left the scene.

\*\*\*

Wayne sat in his mansion talking to his lawyer Mr. Goldberg. From the look on Wayne's face, Mr. Goldberg knew that the man didn't like what he was telling him.

"Listen," Wayne stated plainly, as he poured himself a glass of wine. "I don't give a fuck about none of that shit you just told me. Bottom line is, I have lots of money that I need cleaned," he paused. "And it's your job to clean it."

"I understand that Wayne, but the problem is you have too much money," Mr. Goldberg told him. "Now if you want me to clean it, I'm going to have to charge you more. This is not an easy job."

Wayne knew that Mr. Goldberg worked hard for him and his crew. He also knew the Jewish man wasn't dumb enough to try and cross him. Therefore, he decided to pay the extra. "If I ever go broke, you're the first person I'm coming to, to borrow some money." Wayne laughed as he saw Capo and Moose walking down the long hallway heading towards him.

"Let's wrap this up," Wayne said as he and Mr. Goldberg shook hands.

"Call me tomorrow."

"Will do," Mr. Goldberg said as he stood up and made his exit.

"Yo," Capo said stopping Mr. Goldberg in the hallway. "I appreciate how you got my girl off the hook when they kicked in her door last month."

"Don't mention it," Mr. Goldberg said patting Capo on the back as he continued to the exit. He was one of the best lawyers in New York.

Mr. Goldberg had no problem doing whatever it took to get the job done, even if it meant going under the table to get it done.

"I hope you got good news for me," Wayne said as he watched Capo and Moose help themselves to a seat.

"Yes and no," Capo answered. Immediately, when Wayne heard Capo say yes and no, he knew he had did some wild shit. "What you mean yes and no? It's either yes or no," Wayne said.

"Max didn't have the money so I killed him," Capo said. "But his girl and her mother was there."

"And?" Wayne asked looking at Capo.

"And I let them live," Capo said putting his hands up in the air. "Hold on let me explain," he said knowing he had fucked up. "The bitch said she was willing to work off Max's debt so I figured we could use her to make those out of town trips for us."

"And what happens if she goes to the police?" Wayne asked.

"Fuck the police!" Capo countered. "We got the NYPD in our pocket!"

# THE TEFLON QUEEN

"We got em in our pocket, but that shit cost money Capo," Wayne huffed. "Next time just kill everybody!" Wayne knew Capo was a loose cannon, but the young man was a beast when it came to laying somebody down so he gave him chance after chance. Not to mention he knew Capo from when he was a little shorty. "You keep on acting up and Imma have to get somebody to replace you," Wayne told him.

Capo laughed as he waved him off. "Can't nobody do my job. That's why it's my job!"

"Well if you want to keep your job then you better act like you need it," Wayne said seriously. He loved Capo like a son but he didn't love him enough to risk his own freedom.

"I got everything under control," Capo said confidently.

"We'll see," Wayne said pouring himself another drink. He was going to give Capo one last job, just to see if he could handle it responsibly. If not, he would have to find something else for the man to do. "Listen up," he said. "I need you to go down to Ms. Gina's restaurant tomorrow and pick up what she got for me."

"I got you," Capo replied.

"And do it quietly please," Wayne reminded him.

"Stop worrying so much," Capo said as he and Moose got up and made their exit.

# CHAPTER 2

Shekia relocated to her aunt's house in hopes that the men who had killed Max wouldn't find her. She didn't know the men who murdered Max, but she had seen them around all the time. Shekia thought about just saying fuck it and going to the police, but since she was from the hood, that no snitching mentality was in her veins. Shekia took the time to weigh her options. They had to either do what they told her to do, or go to the cops and pay the price if they ever caught her.

"Fuck it," she said as she pulled out her cell phone and dialed the number that Capo had written down on the small piece of paper. On the fifth ring, someone finally answered. "Who this?"

"Hey this is Shekia," she said nervously. "I'm trying to reach Capo."

"Shekia who?" Capo asked suspiciously thinking that she was a new girl he had met and forgot her name.

"I'm the girl from the other night," Shekia told him. "You shot my boyfriend Max, remember?"

"Oh yeah," Capo said suddenly remembering who she was. "What's good? You ready to get to work?"

"Yes. I want to get this over with as soon as possible," Shekia said.

"A'ight bet. I'm about to text you the address for you to meet me. Meet me at nine o'clock tonight and you better be there," Capo said hanging up in Shekia's ear.

Once he hung up, he immediately texted her the address to the meeting location, as he pulled up in front of Ms. Gina's restaurant.

Capo hopped out his Benz with no shirt on, his pants sagging, two chains around his neck, and a bottle of Rosay in his hand. He quickly slipped his .380 in his pocket as he entered the restaurant. "Damn it feels good in here," Capo huffed as he felt the cool air from the air conditioner hit his body as soon as he stepped foot in the restaurant.

"Excuse me sir," a waiter said politely as he walked up to Capo.

"What's up?" Capo asked as he turned up the bottle and took a long sip.

"Umm you can't come in here with alcohol and you have to have a shirt on if you would like to get served," the waiter told him.

"Listen," Capo said looking at the waiter as the thought of smacking the shit out of him crossed his mind. "Go tell Ms. Gina that somebody is here to see her," he said taking another sip from his bottle. "And tell her don't have me waiting all day either."

Five minutes later, Ms. Gina came downstairs with a frown on her face. "The next time you come into my place of business, make sure you have a shirt on!" Ms. Gina said sternly as she escorted Capo upstairs to her office.

Once the two got inside her office, Ms. Gina slammed the door. "I'm going to call Wayne as soon you leave," she yelled. "I refuse to continue to give my hard earned money to you people!"

"Fuck you mean, you people?" Capo asked feeling offended.

"I'm a classy woman and I expect to do business with someone with at least a little bit of class!" she said looking Capo up and down with a disgusted look on her face. Ms. Gina couldn't stand Capo and every time he came to the restaurant, it was always something and she was sick of it.

"Just give me what you got for me so I can be on my way," Capo said with an attitude. Ms. Gina sucked her teeth as she opened up her safe and roughly placed the brown paper bag in his hand.

"Do I have to count this?" Capo asked with a smirk on his face.

"Fuck you!" Ms. Gina cursed as she watched Capo exit her office.

Before he was fully out of her office, Ms. Gina was already on the phone with Wayne.

When Capo left Ms. Gina's restaurant, he headed straight downtown to go pick up one his shooters named Bone. Bone was an ignorant, loud talking young man with a happy trigger finger. Whenever Bone got around Capo, he would always like to show off in front of him to prove he was the real deal and down for whatever. Bone looked up to Capo and at times, he tried to be just like him. All of the young gangsters wanted to be like Capo.

Capo pulled up to the corner that he owned and hopped out the Benz. "What's good out here?" he asked giving each man dap.

"Ain't shit," Bone replied. "Chasing this paper as usual," he said looking over both shoulders for any trace of cops.

"I'm about to go get some haze. Come take a ride with me," Capo said hopping back in his Benz. Once Bone hopped in, Capo pulled off. "I really needed to holla at you and I didn't want the rest of them niggaz to hear," Capo said slowing down for the yellow light. "How's everything been going on the block?"

"Everything's been good," Bone answered. "I've been keeping everybody in line."

"That's what I like to hear," Capo said smiling. "You keep up the good work and I might think about promoting you."

"You already know," Bone said as he noticed Capo pull over.

"Yo. Wait right here. I'll be right back," Capo said as he hopped out the car and disappeared inside the building in front of where he had parked.

Inside the building, Capo took the steps to the second floor. He came out the staircase and knocked on the door closest to the elevator. Seconds later, a tall ugly brother answered the door. "What's up Capo?"

"Nigga get the fuck out my way, that's what's up," Capo said looking at the ugly man as if he was crazy.

"My bad Capo," the ugly guy apologized.

"Lemme get two ounces before I have to crack your head open in here," Capo said shaking his head while he counted out his money.

The ugly guy quickly went to the back room and returned two minutes later. "You need me to weigh it for you?"

"Nah just gimme that shit so I can get up outta here," Capo said snatching the two ounces out of his hand and stuffing them in his draws as he exited the apartment.

"Bitch ass nigga," the ugly guy said once Capo had left. He couldn't stand Capo, but he just stayed quiet to avoid unnecessary problems with the man.

# SILK WHITE

Capo got back downstairs and hopped back in his Benz. "I'mma need you to put in some work real quick," he said looking over at Bone.

"What's the word?" Bone asked ready for whatever.

"I need you to go upstairs and rob that ugly ass clown that sells the bud," Capo told him. "Just bring me the weed and you can keep the money."

"Say no more," Bone said as he slid out the passenger seat and entered the building. The ugly guy sat on the couch watching Sports Center when he heard a knock at the door. He got up, walked over to the door, and looked through the peephole. The ugly guy saw Bone standing on the other side and immediately opened the door.

"Yo did Capo just come up here?" Bone asked.

"Yeah you just missed him," the ugly guy answered.

"Fuck it just let me get an ounce since I'm already here," Bone said as he stepped inside and started counting some money. Once he saw the ugly guy go to the back room to get the weed, Bone quickly put his money back in his pocket and pulled out his .38.

"You need me to weigh it for you?" the ugly guy asked as he returned to the living room only to find Bone pointing a gun in his face. "You already know what this is," Bone said roughly grabbing the ugly guy by his collar and forcing him back into the back room. "I'm only asking this once," Bone said turning him around so the two men were facing each other. "Put everything in that bag right there," he said nodding to the empty bag that lay on the floor. Bone watched as the ugly guy stuffed about nine pounds of haze in the bag, followed by a few stacks of money.

"Here this all I got," the ugly guy said handing Bone the bag. Bone snatched the bag from his hand and then turned and shot him in the leg.

# THE TEFLON QUEEN

When Bone returned back downstairs, he just smiled at Capo as he hopped back in the Benz.

# CHAPTER 3

Wayne hung up his office phone just as Capo entered his office. Immediately, Capo could tell something was wrong just by the look on Wayne's face. "What's wrong?"

"I just got word that one of Sammy's boys got locked up right after we did the deal with them," Wayne told him.

"Fuck!" Capo cursed. "You think they're going to talk?"

"I don't know," Wayne replied. "But I'm not about to take that chance," he said pouring himself a drink. "I need you to take out whoever you can from Sammy's crew."

Wayne liked Sammy, but not enough to sit in jail for the rest of his life. Therefore, Sammy's crew had to go, point blank period. Wayne and Sammy did business occasionally so the decision wasn't a hard one for Wayne to make.

"I'll get right on it," Capo said as he handed Wayne the money that Ms. Gina had given him.

"Ms. Gina called me earlier complaining about you as usual," Wayne informed him.

"Man fuck her!" Capo said waving him off. "She needs to be thankful I don't just slap the shit out of her."
Wayne just shook his head at how ignorant Capo was. His wild actions were starting to mess up business and if that continued, Wayne was sure to have to do something about it. "The least you can do is put on a shirt when you go into her restaurant," Wayne huffed.

# THE TEFLON QUEEN

"Put a shirt on...," Capo said, sipping on his drink. "These motherfuckers are paying us for protection for a reason and that reason is because we can protect them. Fuck if I have a shirt on or not!"

"You've been bringing a lot of heat down on our crew and our operation," Wayne told him. "Now I need you to calm down and stop being so damn flashy. That's not good for business. Remember I'm the boss and you're the underboss!" he yelled.

"I'll tone it down some," Capo said as he heard his cell phone ringing. "Hello?" he answered.

"Hey what's up? It's me Shekia," the woman on the other end of the phone said. "I'm at the address you told me to meet you at. Where you at?"

"Wait right there ma, I'll be there in ten minutes," Capo said hanging up in her ear. Capo stood up and finished off the rest of his drink. "You want me to tone it down a notch? Then you got it," he said as he turned and left Wayne's office.

\*\*\*

Capo pulled up to the lounge that he owned and pulled into his parking spot. He was still upset that Wayne had tried to scold him. To Capo, Wayne was starting to turn soft and he was not fit to be the leader any longer. Capo had already started building up his team and operation. Even though he thought Wayne was turning soft, his loyalty towards the man was what stopped him from killing Wayne. When Capo didn't have a dime, it was Wayne who had looked out for him. That reason alone was why Wayne's name wasn't on Capo's hit list. He hopped out his Benz and immediately spotted Shekia standing out front. "What's good ma?" Capo said with a smile.

"What's up my ass," Shekia said sucking her teeth. "I've been standing out here waiting for you for over an hour!"

"My bad," Capo said nonchalantly as he escorted her inside the lounge. "Send me a bottle of Rosay to my table," he said tapping one of his servants on the back. "Glad you came," he said as he led Shekia to a small booth in the back of the lounge. In the booth sat Moose, Bone, and girl named Kim. This was Capo's crew. "Have a seat," Capo said as he gave Bone and Moose dap and kissed Kim on her cheek.

"Who the fuck is this bitch?" Kim asked grilling Shekia.

"This here is Shekia," Capo announced. "And she is the newest member on our team."

"I don't know son," Bone protested. "She doesn't look like a rider."

"She has a debt to pay off," Capo said looking at Shekia. "And she's here to work."
"What is it that you need me to do?" Shekia asked nervously. She prayed it wasn't anything too serious like shooting someone or murdering someone. Capo popped open the bottle of Rosay before replying. "All I need you to do is go to Miami at least twice a month, pick up a package, and bring it back."

"You want me to transport drugs from Miami back to New York for you?" Shekia asked.

"Yeah that's exactly what you're going to do," Capo said pausing mid-sip.

"What happens if I get caught?" Shekia asked nervously. Bone, Moose, and Kim immediately busted out laughing.

"You not going to get caught ma," Capo told her. "I already got everything all mapped out," he said sliding her a drink. "Get that in your system and relax."

# THE TEFLON QUEEN

"I don't know about this," Shekia said not liking how the plan sounded. She had never done anything like this in her life and the fear of getting caught was eating away at her. She wasn't the type of girl who could survive in jail.

"Listen," Capo began. "When you in this family, you are protected. You have nothing to worry about."

"Either you in or you out," Kim said tired of playing with the girl.

"I'm in," Shekia announced afraid that if she didn't agree to the terms that she would be killed just like her boyfriend.

"Okay, your first drop off will be in two weeks," Capo told her.

"Okay you got my number," Shekia said as she stood up to leave.

"You're leaving already?" Capo asked. "You don't want to party and enjoy yourself tonight?"

"No thank you," Shekia said as she quickly exited the lounge.

"I don't trust that bitch," Kim said as she watched Shekia exit the lounge.

"You don't trust anybody," Capo said laughing and shaking his head.

Kim got her name because she looked just like the rapper Lil Kim from her face down to her body. Over time, the name just kind of stuck with her. The real reason that she didn't want Shekia down on the team was because she was afraid that Capo would fuck her if the opportunity presented itself. Kim and Capo weren't a couple, but they were in a relationship. It was a friend with benefits kind of relationship.

## SILK WHITE

"I'm just saying we all have a lot to lose if this chick decides to get cold feet."

"She's going to work out fine," Capo said as he saw someone who was down with Sammy's organization walk up into his lounge.

"What's up with this nigga Wayne?" Moose asked. "When you going to tell him you doing your own thing?"

"When the time is right," Capo said staring at the man from Sammy's crew. "Wayne put the hit out on anyone from Sammy's crew," he announced.

There go one of those clowns right there," Bone pointed out ready to make a move.

"You and Moose handle that clown and get up with me tomorrow," Capo said as he and Kim got up and left.

\*\*\*

Once outside, Capo noticed that Kim still had an attitude. "What's your problem?"

"I don't like that new girl," Kim said once the two were alone. Capo knew that Kim's jealous ways were kicking in. He could tell by the way that she was looking at Shekia.

"We'll talk about that later," Capo said not wanting to have that conversation with Kim right now. He just wanted to enjoy the rest of his night. "Meet me at my crib," Capo said as he watched Kim hop in her all-white Lexus.

\*\*\*

# THE TEFLON QUEEN

Back inside the lounge, Bone and Moose sat in the booth finishing off the bottle of Rosay as they watched their target mingle and two-step on the dance floor. "When he goes to the bathroom, we gonna take him out," Bone said helping himself to another drink.

Moose was ready to go home so he prayed the target went to the bathroom soon. He was actually thinking about pushing his shit back in the middle of the dance floor.

Twenty minutes later, the target finally headed towards the bathroom. Immediately, Bone and Moose followed the target into the bathroom. Once inside, Bone pulled out his .38 and kicked in the door to the stall that the target was in. Inside the target sat on the toilet sniffing some white when the stall door busted open. Before he could even say a word, Bone emptied all six of his bullets into the man. Pow! Pow! Pow! Pow! Pow! Pow! Once he was done, Moose came in and pumped five more shots into the man's body. The two exited the restroom and the lounge as if nothing had ever happened.

*\*\**

Back at Capo's house, he and Kim relaxed in his Jacuzzi sipping on some wine. Capo let the jets massage his body while he thought about how and when he planned on telling Wayne that he had his own operation going on. Capo didn't want to seem like he was disloyal, but he was tired of Wayne complaining about how he handled business. Capo's motto was that killers only respected other killers. Capo may not have been liked by everyone, but he was damn sure respected. In Wayne's world, he'd rather talk about things first and in Capo's world, he let his gun do the talking for him.

"What you over there thinking about?" Kim said breaking Capo's concentration as she glided over in his arms.

"Wayne," Capo answered honestly.

"When are you going to tell him?"

"Not sure yet," Capo said taking a sip from his wine glass.

Kim could see that this situation was really eating at Capo so she decided to lighten up the mood. "Don't worry about that tonight baby," Kim said as she turned up the volume to the music with the remote that rested on the side of the tub. Instantly, the sound of Young Jeezy could be heard out by his pool and Jacuzzi area.

"You better not be thinking about Wayne with all this in your face," Kim said as she turned around and began bouncing her ass in and out of the water.

Capo smiled as he smacked Kim's ass. "Come here," he demanded as he stood up and finished his glass of wine.

Kim glided over towards Capo. Since he was standing up, his dick was hanging directly in her face. Kim quickly placed her hair in a bun as she looked in Capo's eyes while she worked him into stiffness with both of her hands. "Who's your bottom bitch?"

"You are baby," Capo replied as he watched Kim go to work. Kim placed Capo's whole dick in her mouth and looking up at him the whole time while she moaned loudly. Capo placed his hand on the back of her head and guided Kim's head to the perfect speed. Kim sucked on Capo's dick like a porno star. "You like that daddy?" she purred as she pushed Capo down back into the water. She kissed Capo on the lips as she straddled him.
"I missed you," Kim whispered in Capo's ear as she reached back and slid Capo's tool inside of her. "Ahhhh," she moaned as she bounced up and down on top of Capo as water splashed all over the place. Capo quickly lifted Kim up off of him as he exploded in the water.

# CHAPTER 4

Capo cruised down one of Sammy's blocks. Young Jeezy's, "Lose My Mind" could be heard as the Benz pulled up to the corner. Capo hopped out the car and walked up to the Spanish men that stood on the corner.

"What up?" Capo greeted the men. "Where's Sammy?" Nobody said a word. All the men just looked at Capo as if they had never heard Sammy's name before.

"A'ight," Capo said with a smirk on his face as he turned and hopped back in his Benz and pulled off. Seconds later, Bone rode pass on a motorcycle. Kim sat backwards on the back of the bike holding an Uzi. "Let's do this shit!" Bone yelled over the engine as he sped up. Once the bike reached the corner, Kim squeezed the trigger on the Uzi as she watched the men on the corner fall like dominos as Bone bent the corner on the bike.

\*\*\*

Wayne sat in his office staring a hole through Capo and Moose.

"What's the problem now?" Capo asked in an uninterested tone. "You told me to take out Sammy's men!"

"I told you do it quietly," Wayne said shaking his head in disgust.

"How many times do I have to keep telling you the same thing over and over again?"

"Listen," Capo said sitting up in his chair. "If you think you can do a better job, then by all means feel free to lead by example!" Capo wanted to tell Wayne to stop acting like a bitch, but he decided to hold his tongue.

"Capo don't play with me!" Wayne warned.

Wayne may not have killed a lot of people himself, but he had paid for the murder of many of men. His money was long so therefore he didn't have to go out a kill somebody with whom he had a problem. All he had to do was pay someone like Capo to handle all of his dirty work.

"So what is it that you want me to do?" Capo asked.

"Just tone it down a bit," Wayne huffed massaging the bridge of his nose. "The heat that's been coming down on me because of these murders has been unbelievable," he said as he stood up. "I have a meeting with Mr. Goldberg right now," Wayne laughed. "This damn lawyer is the only one benefiting off of these murders."

Wayne's personal bodyguard, Tank, shadowed his every move.

"After I come back from Mr. Goldberg's office I think I'm going to come back home and relax," Wayne said as he headed outside.

Outside, his all-black Suburban was waiting in the front like always.

"Make sure you call me later," Wayne said looking at Capo. "And remember…"
"Yeah I know tone it down," Capo said finishing off Wayne's sentence for him.

Before Wayne could say another word, Tank quickly tackled him to the ground as a loud series of gunshots lit up the streets. The sound of tires screeching quickly followed.

# THE TEFLON QUEEN

Capo quickly hopped up and returned fire at the car before the car disappeared around the corner.

At that moment, the "tone it down" talk went straight out the window.

Whoever had just tried to take their life would have to pay with their own, Capo thought as he tucked his .380 back into his waistband. "You still want me to tone it down?" Capo chuckled. Wayne ignored that last comment as he and Tank hopped in the Suburban and peeled off.

"How you want to handle this?" Moose asked looking at Capo.

"You already know how," Capo smirked as he and Moose hopped in his Benz and broke out.

\*\*\*

During the ride to Mr. Goldberg's office, Wayne was silent. All that was on his mind was staying out of jail. Wayne already had two charges pending against him and all the heat that had been coming down on him wasn't helping one bit. Wayne hated how Capo handled business, but he loved the result. All he wished was for Capo to handle things a little more quietly, but deep down inside he knew that Capo wouldn't be able to tone it down. There was only one way that Capo knew how to be and that was loud. Wayne was going to have to do something about the heat that Capo was bringing down on him and his clock was ticking so he was going to have to think of something quick. The Suburban pulled up in the parking spot in front of Mr. Goldberg's. Wayne hopped out and power walked to the entrance of the building with Tank close on his heels.

"Hi, how are you doing?" Wayne said politely to the secretary that sat behind the desk. "Can you tell Mr. Goldberg that Wayne is here to see him?"

"One second please," the secretary replied politely as she watched Wayne and Tank go take a seat in the waiting area.

"So what you wanna do about Capo?" Tank asked.

"Not sure yet," Wayne said as he saw the secretary signal that it was okay for them to go in Mr. Goldberg's office. Wayne and Tank walked in the office and helped themselves to a seat. "How are we looking?" Wayne asked sighing loudly.

"Believe it or not, you are looking pretty good," Mr. Goldberg told him.

"We're going to beat the murder charge thanks to Capo taking out the star witness and they don't have enough evidence to convict you on that drug charge so you're good," Mr. Goldberg said with a smile.

"However," he continued. "After you beat these charges the government and the feds are really going to be coming for your head so what we need to do is come up with a solution to keep you out of trouble and your name out of shit!"

"Easier said than done," Wayne said as the trio erupted with laughter.

"Anything that Capo does my name is automatically brought up."

"So what are we going to do about this?" Mr. Goldberg asked. He too knew that Capo was a loose cannon and if he continued on the path that he was going down, neither him nor Wayne would have their freedom for much longer.

"I have no idea," Wayne said massaging his temples. "I told him time and time again to try to tone it down. I just don't think he can."

# THE TEFLON QUEEN

"I say you need to just cut that clown loose," Tank said straight up.

"I never liked him anyway!"

"Nah," Wayne said. "He paid his dues to play this game." Even though Capo was a pain in the ass, he had saved Wayne's ass and his life on several occasions.

"I have an idea, but I'm going to be honest with you. It's a long shot," Mr. Goldberg announced.

"What did you have in mind?" Wayne whispered.

"I had this one client that introduced me to this hitman, or hit woman I should say, named Angela, also known as the Teflon Queen."

"I heard of her," Wayne said. "She's from Miami right?"

"Yup," Mr. Goldberg replied. "Hire her on your team and she'll be sure to keep Capo in line. Angela don't play no games. She strictly about her business."

"Set me up with a meeting with her a.s.a.p.," Wayne said as he and Mr. Goldberg shook hands.

\*\*\*

"No mommy put the phone down!" Shekia yelled as she wrestled with her mother to hang up the phone.

"No daughter of mine is going to transport drugs!" Ms. Pat barked.

"Mommy it's either do this or they will kill the both of us," Shekia said unplugging the entire phone.

24

"The cops will protect us Kia," Ms. Pat told her.

"Fuck the police!" Shekia cursed. "The police ain't ever helped nobody. Just chill out, I got everything under control. Besides, it's only a few trips."

"It starts out with a few trips," Ms. Pat said as tears streamed down her face. She wanted so badly to call the cops, but she also remembered how they had found Max and what they had done to him.

Ms. Pat knew that even if she told Shekia no, she wasn't going to listen. All she could do was pray for her baby. "Please promise me you are going to be careful?"

"I got you mommy," Shekia said as she hugged her mother tightly. She too was nervous and afraid, but she couldn't let her mother see her like that. She had to stay strong until the storm was over, but how long would the storm last was the question… Shekia pulled out her cell phone and dialed Capo's number. On the fourth ring he finally answered, "Yo?"

"Hey what's up? It's me," Shekia said. "We was supposed to meet up today," she reminded him.

"I'm right outside," Capo replied as he beeped the horn.

"Wait I didn't have a chance to pack yet," Shekia said nervously.

"No need for all that baby," Capo said smoothly. "Just come outside."

Shekia grabbed her purse and kissed her mother on the cheek. "I'll be back in a few days and I promise everything is going to be fine," she said running out the door. Shekia hopped in the passenger seat of the Benz and strapped on her seat belt.

# THE TEFLON QUEEN

"Relax," Capo smiled as he pulled off and headed for the airport.

"Okay so how does this work?" Shekia asked as she looked out the window.

"Simple," Capo replied smoothly. "All you have to do is get on the plane and go to Miami and when you get there dial this number," he said handing her a little piece of paper with a number scribbled down on it.

Shekia took the paper and looked down at it. "Hold up! There's no name on this paper!"

"You don't need a name. All you have to do is call the number," Capo said as if it was no big deal. He knew Shekia was nervous and scared, but he also knew she was perfect for the job. "Relax," he told her as he stopped at a red light. "This is going to be the easiest job you've ever done."

"I want to believe you, but my gut is telling me otherwise," Shekia said sarcastically. She didn't know why, but for some strange reason she trusted Capo and felt comfortable around him. It was the confident way that he spoke, as if he owned the whole world that made her comfortable around the stranger. "I'm trusting you," she said out loud.

"Listen. This is going to be a piece of cake," Capo said as he pulled up to the passenger drop off spot at the airport. "Here," he said as he handed her five thousand dollars. "Go shopping while you out there just in case you get pulled over. At least you'll have some bags in the trunk."

Shekia took the money and slid it in her purse as she slid out the Benz. "If something goes wrong or doesn't feel right can I call you?" Shekia asked sticking her head through the passenger's window.

"You can call me anytime," Capo said with a wink. "Handle your Business," he said as he pulled off.

*** 

Capo pulled into his parking spot at his lounge and cut the engine off as he hopped out and headed towards the entrance. As he got closer to the entrance, he noticed two men who stood in front of the lounge standing out. Their white skin and trench coats gave away their identity as soon as Capo spotted them. Capo could spot a cop from a mile away.

"Hey what's up Capo," one of the detectives said with a smirk on his face.

"Fuck y'all want?" Capo asked in a bored tone as he gave the two bouncers who guarded the front door some dap.

"We just want to have a few drinks and a couple of words with you," the other detective spoke up.

"I don't talk to pigs," Capo said causing the two bouncers to bust out laughing. "So if I'm not under arrest then y'all can kiss my ass," he said entering the lounge. "Motherfuckers," he mumbled under his breath. Capo looked behind him and saw the detectives enter the lounge. "This is harassment," Capo said as he pulled out his cell phone and snapped a picture of the two detectives.

"Harassment my ass," the taller detective out of the two said and brushed Capo off by waving his hand in the air. "This lounge is open to the public right?"

"We just here to have a few drinks and enjoy ourselves," the shorter detective said as the two headed over to the bar. Capo just shook his head as he made his way over to his booth in the back of the lounge.

# THE TEFLON QUEEN

"We got company," he announced nodding over to the bar.

"Somebody snitching," Kim blurted out.

"Nah we just hot right now," Capo said pouring himself a drink.

"So what's the plan?" Bone asked never taking his eyes off the two white men that sat at the bar looking suspicious and out of place.

"Same plan. We going to continue to get this money," Capo told him.

"They don't have anything on us because if they did we would be in cuffs right now. They just fishing right now," he said as he answered his ringing cell phone. "Yo?"

"I need you in my office right now. We need to talk," Wayne said ending the call not trying to be disrespectful, but he just didn't like to talk on the phone. "Imma catch up with y'all later. I gotta go see Wayne real quick," he said as he stood up.

"When you plan on telling him?" Moose asked.

"The end of the month," Capo said as he headed for the exit.

# CHAPTER 5

Capo pulled up in Wayne's driveway and he immediately knew Wayne wasn't alone by the red Lamborghini sitting in the driveway. Wayne would never be caught driving a car like that. He always said it was too flashy and a police magnet. "This motherfucker is nice," Capo said to himself as he looked at the car for a few seconds before heading for the front door. Capo rang the doorbell and waited patiently for a response.

"What's up?" Tank greeted as he opened the door and stepped to the side so Capo could enter.

"Where the big man at?" Capo asked walking through the mansion as if he was the owner.

"In the office," Tank replied as he followed Capo back into the office. Capo stepped in Wayne's office and saw a beautiful woman sitting at the table alongside Wayne. The woman wore an all-white tight fitting business suit to go along with the all-white pumps that she wore on her feet. The woman favored the actress Angelina Jolie, but with a tan. Capo had to stop himself from staring. "Capo have a seat," Wayne said as he poured three drinks. He handed one to Angela and slid one over to Capo. "Angela, this is Capo. Capo, this here is Angela, but you might know her better as the Teflon Queen."

"You're the Teflon Queen?" Capo asked with a smirk on his face.

"Yes I am," Angela replied. "Why is something funny?"

"Nothing," Capo said. "I just heard so many stories about you and I just didn't expect for you to look the way you do."

# THE TEFLON QUEEN

Angela remained silent as she sipped on her drink and continued to stare a hole through Capo.

"Angela is here to help out with the enforcing," Wayne said.

"Fuck you mean here to help out with the enforcing," Capo barked. "Enforcing is my job!"

"I said she's here to help out with the enforcing, not replace you," Wayne said. He knew Capo wasn't going to like his decision, but that's why he was the boss and Capo was the underboss.

"I don't need her help," Capo raved.

"Apparently you do," Angela said. "All of the heat that's been coming down on this whole organization is because of you and your Wild West cowboy antics."

"I know you ain't talking," Capo said looking at Angela. "Your name is buzzing from coast to coast, but I'm the wild cowboy?"

"My name might be buzzing, but yet I can walk into any police station in America and nobody will know who I am. Can you do that?"

Wayne sat back and let the two get out whatever the two had on their chest. He hated to have to be the bad guy, but this decision was a necessary one. "Alright that's enough!" Wayne said ending the two's argument. "Angela is a part of the team now and that's final. Her job is just to help you do your job a little more quietly."

"Fuck you Wayne!" Capo growled. "I've been nothing but good to you. Now you want to come and bring in some outsider, a motherfucker we don't even know into our operation? Fuck you!" he huffed as he stood up to leave.

## SILK WHITE

"What's wrong? You think I'm going to come in and do your job better then you?" Angela taunted.

"You wish you could do a better job than me," Capo smirked.

"Capo sit down," Wayne said pouring himself another drink. "Angela is in the family now and that's final. Do you have a problem with that?"

"Nah," Capo answered sourly.

"Good," Wayne said. "I need the two of you to go and get rid of two of Sammy's men over at their stash place."

"And where's this stash place located?" Capo asked

"Over at that pool hall downtown," Wayne said as he watched the two get up and leave.

\*\*\*

"We're taking my car," Capo said with an attitude as hopped in his Benz. "Just sit down, be quiet, and don't touch nothing," he huffed as he zoomed out of the driveway burning rubber.

For the entire ride, the two didn't say a word to the other one. They just cruised as the sound of Jay-Z filled the car. Capo couldn't believe that Wayne had gone behind his back and hired the Teflon Queen. To Capo that was like a slap in the face. *"Fuck it! Once this month is over I'm telling that nigga I want out anyway!"* Capo thought as he pulled up in front of the pool hall.

"When we get in there let me do all the talking," Capo said as he tucked his .45 in his waistband as the two hopped out the car and entered the pool hall. Inside the pool hall, three Spanish men sat around talking.

"Hey, we're closed," one of the Spanish men, barked!

# THE TEFLON QUEEN

"Motherfucker, does it look like we here to play pool?" Capo replied matching the Spanish man's tone. Just as Capo was about to make a move, Angela quickly zipped out her .380 with the silencer on it and fired three shots. She then placed her gun back in its holster. When Capo looked up, he saw all three men sprawled out on the floor.

*"What the fuck?"* He thought as he walked over towards the three dead bodies.

"Go find the stash!" Angela barked as she closed the front door and locked it. While Capo searched the place for the stash, Angel made sure she checked the pulse on each man making sure they were as dead as a doorknob. This was the only way Angela knew how to move, quietly, and violently. In and out was her trademark and so far she had never missed a target, and she didn't plan on doing such a thing no time soon.

"Bingo!" Capo said as he returned from the back holding a suitcase in his hand.

When the two got back in the car, Capo glanced over at Angela. He liked her style and it turned him on that she could just kill a person as if it was nothing. Of course, he would never tell her this. He didn't really like her, but he had no choice but to respect her.

# CHAPTER 6

As soon as Shekia's foot stepped off the plane, she could instantly feel the butterflies in her stomach. A million thoughts ran through her mind, such as what would happen if she got caught by the police? What if whoever she was here to meet tried to kidnap her? Shekia looked at the piece of paper with the number scribbled down on it about ten times before she finally dialed the number.

"Hello?" she said when she heard somebody on the other end pick up.

"What's up?" a deep voice boomed through the receiver.

"Umm I'm here," Shekia said and suddenly the line went dead. *"What the fuck?"* she thought to herself. Just as she readied to dial Capo's number, Shekia felt a hand tap her on her shoulder. When she turned around, she saw a man with dread locks that came down to the middle of his back and a mouth full of gold teeth. "Shekia right?" Gold Teeth asked.

"Yeah," Shekia nodded.

"My name is Scarface," he said as he headed outside to where his car was parked. Shekia kept her mouth shut and followed the man back to his car. Outside, Scarface hopped in an all-white Range Rover.

"Ma relax! I'm not going to hurt you," Scarface smiled as he started up the vehicle and pulled off. "So is this your first time in Miami?"

"Yeah I'm a city girl," Shekia replied checking out the scenery from the passenger seat.

# THE TEFLON QUEEN

"I'mma have to get you out here more often," Scarface said, openly flirting with the girl who rode shotgun in his Range Rover. Twenty minutes later, Scarface pulled up to a big ass mansion. Outside of the mansion, there stood multiple armed security guards.

"Is this your house?" Shekia asked like a little kid in a candy store.

"Of course it is," Scarface smiled as he hopped out of the Range Rover and walked up to the front of the mansion where he greeted his security. Shekia stood around admiring the house while he spoke. She noticed that he had his own basketball and tennis court over on the side of the mansion. She could also see about three maids walking around the property. Scarface finished talking to his security and directed all of his attention back into Shekia. "Everything will be ready in about an hour," he told her.

"Okay, so like how does this process work?" Shekia asked feeling a little bit more comfortable around the stranger.

"Well it's simple," Scarface began. "I own my own car rental company, so my workers are putting the "stuff" somewhere in the car where it can't be found just in case you have any run-ins with the law," he told her. "So you got about an hour and a half wait. Anything you would like to do?" Immediately, Shekia's mind went to the five gee's that Capo had given her to go shopping. Of course, she wanted to go shopping, but she really needed the money so she decided to hold on to it instead.

"Umm, what is there to do around here?" Shekia asked looking around. Scarface smiled.

"Follow me," he said as he led her inside the mansion. As the two walked through the huge house, Shekia felt as if she had been doing something wrong all her life. Scarface led Shekia through the mansion and out to his backyard.

**SILK WHITE**

"Oh my God," Shekia said as she covered her mouth. She couldn't believe what she was seeing. Scarface's backyard led straight to his private beach.

"You have your own beach?" Shekia asked in shock. Scarface laughed. "I don't have my own beach," he said trying to downplay it. "The beach is open to everyone. I just had this place built like this so it could feel like I had my own beach."

"This is amazing," Shekia said out loud taking in the nice view. Being a girl who never left New York, seeing something like this was simply amazing.

"Follow me," Scarface said as he removed his shirt and threw his dreads in a ponytail. Shekia followed Scarface down to the water to where a Jet Ski rested.

"Oh hell no," Shekia said shaking her head. "No way am I getting on that!"

"Come on. It will be fun," Scarface told her as he began pushing the Jet Ski deeper into the water. "Come on!"

"I don't have a swim suit," she said looking for any excuse not to get on that thing.

"So what," Scarface said looking back at her.

*"Fuck it,"* Shekia said to herself as she stripped down to her bra and thong and ran out into the water and hopped on the back of the Jet Ski with Scarface. As she wrapped her arms around his waist to hold on, she couldn't help but to feel his six-pack. *"Damn!"* She thought as Scarface made the Jet Ski come to life. Shekia held on as tight as she could, closing her eyes as Scarface rode through the ocean like a mad man. Shekia's stomach felt like she was on a roller coaster as she screamed with each bump that the Jet Ski hit.

"Oh my God," Shekia said as she hopped off the Jet Ski. "That was so much fun!"

"Glad you enjoyed yourself," Scarface replied as the two made their way through the sand heading back to the mansion. "You can take a shower before you go," Scarface said nodding towards one of the many bathrooms in the mansion. "After you undress just kick your under clothes out so I can have one of the maids dry them for you."

"Okay," Shekia said not believing how good the day was turning out to be. After her shower, Shekia got dressed and gave Scarface a nice tight warm hug.

"Make sure you call me," Scarface said as he watched Shekia hop in the Camry.

"I got you," Shekia replied with a wink as she pulled off.

\*\*\*

"Just be quiet and don't touch anything," Angela said repeating what Capo had told her when they were in his car. She pulled her Lamborghini out into traffic as if she was racing. Wayne had sent the two on another mission and neither of them were happy about working together again. Capo reached out to touch Angela's radio, but she quickly slapped his hand away. "Didn't I tell you not to touch anything?" she said looking over at Capo as if he was crazy.

"What you know about Rick Ross anyway?" Capo said sucking his teeth. "Are you even black?"

"Yes I am black thank you never much," Angela said rolling her eyes as she cut the volume up while she weaved in and out of traffic. As Angela drove, Capo looked at her beautifully toned legs on the low. *"Damn"* he said to himself as his eyes shifted up to her nice thighs that were also toned very nicely. It was probably from the training her body was used to going through.

"What you looking at?" Angela asked catching Capo's eyes wondering.

"Why you wearing dress clothes?" Capo asked trying to make it seem like he wasn't really checking her out.

"Because I'm a professional, that's why," she replied as they pulled up a block away from their latest victim's house and she placed the car in park.

"Now listen," Capo said turning to face Angela. "Last time I let you run the show. Now it's time for you to see a master at work so take notes." He winked at her as he hopped out the car and headed towards the house. Angela hopped out and walked closely behind him as her heels click clacked loud on the pavement.

"Damn!" Capo huffed with his face crumbled up. "Take them loud ass shoes off!" Angela ignored him as she walked up to the front door and placed her ear against it. She listened for about five seconds before removing a bobby pin from her hair and sticking it inside the key hole on the lock. Just as she was about to pop the lock, Capo kicked the front door open. "Fuck all this waiting shit!" he huffed as he ran up in the house with his .45 drawn. Angela just shook her head as she removed her silenced .380 from its holster and quickly ran inside the house behind Capo with her arms extended with both hands on her weapon.

When Carlos saw his front door kicked open, he quickly got up and attempted to scramble over to the couch where his shotgun rested. A bullet to the back of his thigh immediately canceled that thought as he went crashing through his coffee table.

"Get ya bitch ass up!" Capo growled as he grabbed a chair from out the kitchen, sat it in the middle of the living room, and forced Carlos to sit in it. Capo quickly hand cuffed the man's hands behind his back. Angela walked up to Carlos and looked into his eyes.

"Where's....."

"I got this!" Capo said cutting Angela off as he turned and faced Carlos. "Where the fuck is Sammy at?" he asked.

"Me no speak no English," Carlos said shrugging his shoulders. Capo chuckled as he turned and backslapped Carlos across the face with his gun drawing blood instantly. "You don't know English motherfucker?" Capo yelled as he hit Carlos three more times across the face with the gun. "For the last time! Where can we find Sammy?" Carlos looked up at Capo as if he didn't understand a word he said. Capo looked over at Angela and shook his head as he fired a shot into Carlos's knee. POW!

"Ahhhhhh!" Carlos yelled as pain shot through his whole body.

"Last time," Capo said pressing the smoking hot barrel against Carlos's forehead. Angela sighed loudly as she placed her .380 back in her holster and walked up to Carlos and quickly swept the legs of the chair from up under him causing him to fall straight back onto his back. She placed her feet on Carlos's neck and instantly, a four-inch blade popped out the front of her shoe right on Carlos's neck, just enough to pinch him. "Donde' esta Sammy?" Angela said asking Carlos where Sammy is in Spanish. Carlos quickly answered the question in Spanish. Once Angela had all the information she needed, she smoothly ran the blade effortlessly across Carlos's throat killing him instantly. "Come on lets go," Angela said as the blade went back inside her shoe and she exited the house. Capo smirked as he watched Angela walk out the house. He had to give Angela her props, when it came to getting rid of a victim she didn't play.

"Hold up," Capo said as he jogged and caught up with Angela. Once the two of them were inside the car, Capo looked over at Angela. "How long have you been doing this?"

# SILK WHITE

"Too long," she replied not really answering his question. Angela didn't like to answer questions. She was trained not too. Keeping her mouth closed was instilled in her from when she was a little child.

"Can you teach me that trick you did back there?" Capo asked laughing loudly. Angela ignored Capo's question and turned up the volume on the stereo. Rick Ross' song "Super High" blasted throughout the car as the two rode back to Wayne's place.

\*\*\*

# CHAPTER 7

Shekia smiled brightly when she finally arrived back in New York. Her trip to Miami was one she would not soon forget. For the entire ride back, she thought about Scarface and the great time he had shown her. Shekia hadn't had that much fun in a long time and already she was missing it and him too. *"He probably got a gang of beautiful woman that he could choose from,"* she said to herself trying to talk herself out of thinking about Scarface. Shekia quickly pulled out her cell phone and dialed Capo's number. On the fifth ring he finally answered, "Yo?"

"Where are you?" Shekia asked.

"The lounge," Capo replied. "When you get here call me from the parking lot," he said hanging up in Shekia's ear.

"Rude motherfucker!" Shekia huffed as she tossed her phone on the passenger seat. When she got there, she planned on asking Capo how many more trips she would have to make to pay off the debt that Max had left behind. She popped in her Monica C.D. and sung her heart out while she got her cruise on. Twenty minutes later, Shekia pulled up in the lounge's parking lot, grabbed her cell phone, and dialed Capo's number again.

"You outside?" he asked.

"Yes I'm here!"

"A'ight wait right there. Moose will be there in one second," Capo said hanging up in her ear again. Minutes later, Shekia saw Moose and Kim emerge from the lounge.

# SILK WHITE

"Capo wants to see you inside," Moose said opening Shekia's door. As soon as she got out of the car, Moose hopped in the driver seat and pulled off in the rental.

"Yo come on, I ain't got all day," Kim said with an attitude as she lead the way into the club. Shekia sucked her teeth, but decided to bite her tongue and not stoop down to Kim's level. "She's with me," Kim said, as one of the bouncers got ready to frisk Shekia. When Shekia stepped foot inside the lounge she saw that it was packed like always. When Kim didn't take Shekia to the usual booth that was located in the back, she immediately began to get nervous. *"Where the fuck is she taking me?"* Shekia thought as Kim took her to the back of the lounge where two big bouncers guarded a door. When Kim walked up, the two bouncers immediately stepped to the side so that she and Shekia could enter. Behind that door was a little hallway that lead to another door. Kim reached the door and did a special knock. Seconds later, the door opened up. Inside sat Capo, Bone, and two other goons. In the middle of the floor was a man on his knees.

"Okay now tell me what happened," Capo said as he sat down in his chair looking at the man who was in the middle of the room.

"I heard this bitch ass nigga snitched on you and told Wayne that you were out here doing your own thing," Bone said pointing at the guy in the middle of the room.

"He's fucking lying Capo!" the man on his knees in front of Capo yelled. "I would never do no shit like that" he lied.

"Why the fuck would somebody make up some shit like that?" Bone asked as he turned and stole on the man named Kenny.

"I swear to God, I wasn't the one who snitched," Kenny pleaded.

"Then who was it?" Capo asked in a calm voice. On the outside, he was calm but on the inside, he was furious. Not only was it a chance that

# THE TEFLON QUEEN

Wayne would have him killed for doing some shit like that, but there was also a chance Wayne could try to blackball Capo so he couldn't make any more money in the city and that right there would be the start to World War III.

"I swear it wasn't me," Kenny said crying like a baby. He knew he had fucked up when he went to go snitch on Capo. The $15,000.00 Wayne gave him didn't mean anything now. Capo was about to say something, but was interrupted when he heard his phone ringing. He looked at the caller I.D. and saw Wayne's name flashing across the screen and at that very moment, Capo knew he was in some deep shit. "Yo?" he answered.

"Get your ass to my office NOW!" Wayne yelled before hanging up in Capo's ear. Capo chuckled as he ended the call and slid his phone back into its case. "So," he said as he stood up looking at Kenny. "You wanna go around running your mouth about shit that don't even have nothing to do with you right?"

"Please Capo. I didn't do it. You have to believe me," Kenny pleaded sounding like a bitch.

"Hold this motherfucker down!" Capo ordered as he reached in his desk drawer and removed a large hunting knife. *"Niggaz wanna go out and run they fucking mouth!"* he said to himself as he watched the two goons pin Kenny down to the floor. Shekia stood by the wall and watched in horror as Capo stabbed and cut Kenny up into pieces. After a while, the scene became so graphic that Shekia had to cover up her eyes with her hands. Capo stabbed Kenny until his arm grew tired and he couldn't stab him anymore. "Motherfucker!" he growled as he tossed the knife down on the floor. Capo was so pissed that he wanted to bring Kenny back to life so he could kill him all over again. Everybody watched in silence as Capo went back to his seat and sat down. After about two minutes of silence, Kim finally decided to break the silence.

"So what we gonna do about this Wayne situation?"

"I'm not sure yet," Capo replied. He didn't know what his next move was, but he there was definitely about to be some drama behind what had just went down.

"Well, whatever you decide to do just know I got your back," Kim told him meaning every word.

"I'm about to head over there and see what's popping," Capo said as he stood.

"You want me to come with you?" Bone asked. "I heard that nigga Wayne got this new girl on his team," he paused. "I heard she's the real deal."

"She ain't all that," Capo lied. "I'll be good by myself."

"Be careful," Kim said as she hugged Capo before he left the back room. Capo stepped out the back room and made his way back towards the door that led him inside the lounge. "Boss you alright?" One of the bouncers asked as he noticed Capo's shirt covered in blood.

"It's all good," Capo yelled over his shoulder as he headed to the bar and grabbed a bottle of Rosay before exiting the lounge. "This gonna be a long night," Capo huffed as he took a swig from his bottle and headed outside, hopped in his Benz, and headed towards Wayne's mansion.

Once Capo pulled up he noticed Angela's Lamborghini parked in the parking lot. Capo parked directly behind the Lamborghini. He cut his car off and slid his .45 in his waistband as he hopped out the Benz and made his way to the front door. If you looked at Capo, he seemed regular, but deep down he was nervous and on edge. The last thing he wanted was for Wayne to find out like this. Capo rang the doorbell and waited for someone to answer. Seconds later, one of Wayne's maids answered the door. Capo quickly brushed past the woman as he made his way down the long hallway that led to Wayne's office. He entered Wayne's office without knocking. "What's up?" Capo said as he walked in and helped himself to a seat. Inside the office sat just Wayne and Angela.

"So, this is how we do things now?" Wayne asked staring a hole through Capo. "You thought you could go and do your own thing without me finding out?"

"I was going to tell you," Capo said nonchalantly taking a swig from his bottle. He knew he was busted so he figured why even try to deny it.

"I trusted you," Wayne said with venom in his voice. "Treated you like family. When you were running around here broke, who fed you?"

The look on Capo's face told Wayne that he could care less about what he was saying. "So just because I was working for you, you expect me to work for you forever? Come on with the bullshit, you know I'm my own man and more importantly I'm a hustler," Capo told him.

"Look at this motherfucker," Wayne chuckled as he looked over at Angela. "Motherfucker starts making some money and now he thinks he's Wayne. You think you can do my job?"

"I've been doing it," Capo said cockily while sipping from his bottle. Wayne looked over at Capo with a disgusted look on his face. He couldn't believe that Capo had betrayed him the way he did. "Get the fuck out of my house!" Wayne huffed. "The only reason I'm letting you live is because I still have a little love for you, but if I hear about you or anybody associated with you on any of my corners or interfering with anything that has to do with me, I'm going to send Angela to kill you! Now get the fuck out!"

Capo stood up from his seat and winked at Angela before he left Wayne's office. As he left Wayne's mansion he felt bad about what had just happened. It seemed worse than it really was only because of the way Wayne had found out. *"Fuck it! It is, what it is,"* Capo said to himself as he hopped in his Benz and backed out the driveway.

"You should have let me kill him," Angela said once Capo had left the office.

"Trust me, I thought about it," Wayne said pouring himself another drink. "But right now I have enough problems and I don't need to add to them." The truth was, he still had love for Capo, and although Capo fucked him over, if it wasn't for Capo, Wayne knew he would have either been in jail for the rest of his life by now or dead a long time ago. "What's up with Sammy?" Wayne asked changing the subject.

"I know exactly where he rests his head. I was just waiting on the word from you," Angela stated plainly.

Wayne finished his drink before he replied. "Take care of that clown as soon as possible!"

"No problem," Angela smiled. She was glad that she no longer had to work with Capo. He was cool, but the Teflon Queen worked best alone.

"I want you to come out with me tonight," Wayne said handing Angela the money for the last contract.

"What you mean? To like a party?" Angela asked thumbing through the cash.

"Yes, something like that," Wayne said with a smile. "I just want to show you a good time and show you I appreciate what you've been doing for me."

# THE TEFLON QUEEN

Angela sat and thought about it for a second. Parties and clubs weren't her cup of tea. The last thing Angela wanted was to be around a lot of people, but from the look on Wayne's face she could tell he wasn't going to take no for an answer. "Fuck it lets go."

"Wonderful! Tank is pulling the car around now," Wayne said as he and Angela headed out front door. When the two stepped outside Tank was already in the front waiting for them. "I'm going to show you how to really get your party on," Wayne said excitedly as the two hopped in the all-black Navigator. Once the vehicle was in motion, Wayne looked over at Angela, "So you said you know where to find Sammy at?"

"Yes, I know exactly where to find him," Angela said as she pulled out her .380 with the silencer on it and began taking it apart so she could clean it.

"I want you to pop his brains out of his fucking head when you catch him," Wayne said getting excited at just the mention of Sammy's name.

"Not a problem," Angela replied never looking up from what she was doing. Ten minutes later, Tank pulled up in the club's parking lot and parked over in the reserved parking spot.

"Damn this bitch is packed," Tank said out loud, as the trio hopped out the truck and headed towards the entrance. At the front door, a large bouncer Wayne hired from time to time stood looking like he couldn't wait for somebody to act up.

"Yo, Rodney, what up?" Wayne said giving the big man some dap. As soon as Rodney saw Wayne, he already knew what time it was so he immediately pulled back the rope and allowed the trio to enter the club without being charged or frisked. The trio walked in the club and were immediately treated like royalty by the staff. The owner of the club along with a bouncer escorted the trio to a table. "Let me get a few bottles over here," Wayne ordered as he bobbed his head to the beat that pounded through the speaker. "This is the life right here," Wayne said looking around the club at the other partygoers enjoying themselves. "I work so hard that sometimes I just have to treat myself," he said out loud to no one in particular.

Angela just sat quietly and listened to the music as Wayne and Tank stood trying to talk to a few women over in the corner. Angela sat babysitting a drink when she felt some one tap her on her shoulder.
"Is this seat taken?" a handsome, light skinned man asked nodding at the empty seat next to Angela. Angela looked up at the man and immediately was impressed with his looks. "No, nobody is sitting there," she replied.

"I saw you sitting over here all by yourself so I thought you could use some company," the handsome man said extending his hand. "My name is James," he paused. "James Carter."

"It's nice to meet you Mr. James Carter," Angela said giggling like a child. It had been a while since she heard someone introduce themself giving their first and last name.

"So what brings you out to this club tonight?" James asked as he took a sip from his drink. Angela shrugged. "I didn't have anything else to do, so I just decided to come here to get out the house. How about yourself?"

"Well," James began. "I'm always at work and this weekend is the last one I have off for a while, so I said why not come out and get a drink."

"I feel you," Angela said. "So what do you do for a living?"

James took a sip from his drink before he replied. "I'm a federal agent."

"A federal agent?" Angela echoed. "You mean like the F.B.I?" she asked just trying to make sure she wasn't hearing things.

James chuckled. "Yes is something wrong with that?"

"So you're telling me," Angela said as she turned and faced James. "You work for the F.E.D.S?"

"Yes," James said as he flashed his badge. "I'm one of the top agents in the world," he told her. "You never told me your name," he suddenly remembered.

"My name is not important," Angela said as she got up and walked away. She didn't get far before she felt James grab her by her wrist.

"What's the matter?" James asked. "You don't like cops or something?"

"I hate cops," Angela spat. "All they do is put black men in jail. When in all reality, they are the biggest criminals themselves."

"You are absolutely right," James said. "But I'm not like that. I only take on the big cases and take down people I know for a fact are no good."

"That's what they all say," Angela huffed as she tried to jerk her hand loose.

"Wait," James said as he dug down in his pocket and removed his card and handed it to Angela. "I'm getting ready leave. Promise me you will call me tonight."

Angela looked at James as if he was crazy, but she couldn't deny the fact that he was fine. Talking to James went against everything Angela stood for. She was trained how to survive, change her identity if need be, but talking to James would be a big risk. He was the enemy and she knew it. "Okay I promise I'll call you tonight."

# SILK WHITE

"Thanks," James said flashing his million-dollar smile. "Now what is your name?"

"Angie," Angela said saying the first name that came to her mind. James smiled. "I'm going to be waiting for your call later on," he said as he walked off and disappeared through the crowd.

Angela looked down at James Carter's card and smiled as she slid it inside her pocket. *"I'll just use him for some sex then cut him loose,"* Angela thought as she went over to where Wayne sat and sat next to him.

"Where you been? I was looking for you?" Wayne asked as soon as Angela sat down.

"Over there by the bathroom and some clown was trying to holla at me," Angela said nonchalantly trying to down play how she felt. Ever since he had left, James' face was stuck in her brain. Angela liked him, but she knew that nothing serious would or could ever come out of it because of what he did for a living. As Angela sat bobbing her head to the music, she noticed five Spanish men heading in their direction. Each of the five men's eyes was locked on Wayne. Angela glanced over at Wayne and saw that he and Tank were laughing and both off guard. Angela smoothly slid her .380 out of its holster and rested it on her lap as she continued to watch the five men approach. Once the men got close enough, Angela quickly stomped the leg of Wayne's chair causing him to fall out his seat and out of harm's way. Angela swiftly lifted her arms and fired three shots in rapid secession. "PST! PST! PST!" the three bullets found a home in three of the gunmen's heads, but before Angela could take out the other two gunmen, they had already pulled out automatic weapons and began shooting the place up. She quickly ducked down and took cover as other partygoers who stood next to her and Wayne dropped like flies. Angela aimed her .380 at one of the gunmen's legs as she lay under the table and sent a bullet in each one of his kneecaps. Once the gunman dropped and was in Angela's view, she quickly pulled the trigger putting a bullet in his head, ending the man's

# THE TEFLON QUEEN

career. "Come on we have to go!" Angela yelled as she got up and helped Wayne get to his feet. The two jogged towards the exit blending in with the rest of the crowd who tried to kill one another to get out of harm's way. Angela looked over her shoulder and saw Tank and the last gunman having a shootout as she and Wayne squeezed out the side exit door.

"Don't run! Walk calmly," Angela instructed as she held on to Wayne's arm with one hand while her other hand rested on the handle of her .380 until the two made it their vehicle. Wayne hopped behind the wheel and stormed out of the parking lot. "Sammy has got to go!" Wayne yelled. He was tired of looking over his shoulders every five minutes. Now it was time to eliminate all of his competitors and enemies. "I want him gone first thing tomorrow!" Wayne fumed.

"No problem," Angela replied as she removed the clip from her .380 and replaced it with a fresh one.

"Thanks for holding me down back there," Wayne said glancing over at Angela. "Shit you really are the Teflon Queen," he chuckled meaning every word.

"It's the least I could do," Angela replied with a smile. Even though she was talking to Wayne, her mind was still on James. Angela was always so focused on her jobs that she really didn't have time for men nor did she have time to have a man in her life. The conversation she had with James was a well-needed one. Angela couldn't remember the last time she just had a regular conversation with a man about something other than business.

"What you over there thinking about?" Wayne asked noticing that Angela was staring out into space.

"Just a little tired," she lied and placed a fake smile on her face. Wayne pulled up in his driveway and let the engine die. "You can spend the night here if you like. I have plenty of room if you don't feel like driving anywhere at this time of night," Wayne offered.

"No that's okay," Angela said politely. "I have to get prepared. I got a big day ahead of me tomorrow," she said as she shook Wayne's hand and quickly slid in her Lamborghini and peeled off.

# CHAPTER 8

Now that Capo was all on his own and calling his own shots, his bank account doubled in less than a month's time. The only problem was all of these new fake wannabe hustlers calling themselves trying to compete with him and his organization. Capo cruised around in his Benz with two chains around his neck and no shirt on his back. He cruised around local hoods with Moose in the passenger seat hoping they saw any of the competition out on the streets.

"I wish I would catch a nigga out on one of our corners," Moose said exhaling weed smoke through his nose.

"I been hearing niggaz been out here trying to steal our clientele," Capo said taking the blunt from Moose.

"Yeah, me and Bone ran down on a few of them clowns so we shouldn't be seeing too many of them clowns out here no more," Moose said confidently. The problem was that when Bone put in work, he usually went overboard and that was bringing down more and more heat on Capo's operation.

"Our major problem is all this heat that's been coming down on us," Capo said peeking through his rearview mirror making sure they weren't being followed. Something he always did when he was behind the wheel. "We have to come up with a way to do this shit a little more quietly," Capo said finally realizing what Wayne had been trying to tell him all along.

"So what do you suggest we do?" Moose asked.

"Let's just get this money and enjoy it," Capo replied. "I don't want nobody's head getting busted unless it just has to be done." Just as those words left Capo's mouth, he cruised down the street and saw two young hustlers standing on a corner hustling. From the look of the two kids, they couldn't have been any older then sixteen, maybe seventeen.

"Look at these two chumps," Capo said out loud as he slowed the Benz down stopping right in front of the two teenagers. He rolled down his window and immediately one of the kids walked up to his window.

"I got what you need. Just tell me how you want it," the kid said with a hustlers tongue.

"Nigga, does it look like I use drugs?" Capo said with a smirk on his face. "Who y'all out here working for?"

"Crazy Moe," the young hustler replied.

"How old are you?" Capo asked.

"How old are you?" the young hustler shot back. Capo just smiled as he pulled out his .45 and shot the young hustler in his leg. The other young man tried to take off running but a bullet to the back of his thigh quickly stopped that thought as he hit the ground. "Y'all lil niggaz better stay the fuck off my corners!" Capo yelled as he pulled off. "Lil niggaz got a lot of balls," he said shaking his head as he hopped on the FDR drive highway. "How everything else been moving?"

"Good," Moose replied. "Niggaz really been feeling this new work we got from Scarface. I don't know where he getting his shit from but all I know is, his shit is straight uncut."

"As much money as we paying for that shit it better be uncut," Capo said as he pulled up to one of his stash houses. Now that Capo was on his own and making so much money, he knew soon that he was going to have to beef up his security being as though he couldn't be in twenty different places at one time.

Capo and Moose reached the door and did the special knock. Seconds later, Kim answered the door. "What's up y'all?" she asked stepping to the side so the two could enter. Kim quickly went back behind the table where she sat counting and placing rubber bands over each stack of money that she counted.

"How shit been looking?" Capo asked looking around.

"Everything's been good," Kim answered not bothering to look up from what she was doing. "This new shit got these motherfuckers going crazy," she added.

"That's what I like to hear," Capo said reading a text message that just came through his phone. "How much longer you got to go?" he asked looking over at Kim who was just placing the last rubber band on a neat stack of money. "All done. Why what's up?" Kim asked as she stood up and stretched. She knew whatever Capo had to tell her, it had something to do with some money. She knew that look anywhere.

"I just got the drop on a stash house," Capo announced sliding his phone back in the case that hung on his waist.

"Let's go get that money," Moose said as the trio exited the stash crib.

Once everyone was in the car Capo quickly pulled away from the curb.

"What's up with this Crazy Moe nigga I keep hearing about?" Kim asked from the backseat.

"What you been hearing?" Capo asked keeping his eyes on the road.

"I heard he some new nigga that just came out of nowhere and started opening shop," Kim replied.

# SILK WHITE

"What this nigga look like?" Capo asked eyeing her through the rearview mirror.

"Nah, just heard he been on some real takeover shit," Kim said. "And I heard he rolling with a team of killers. I mean I hear these niggaz putting it in broad daylight and all that."

Capo chuckled as he glanced over at Moose. The look on his face said that he wasn't impressed and neither was Capo. "We gon bump into each other soon," Capo said making the Benz come to a stop. He planned on making an example out of the man the streets called Crazy Moe. Capo was the only name the streets needed to be talking about and he planned to make sure the streets knew exactly whom Capo was.

"If we ain't out in ten you know what to do," Capo said to Kim as he and Moose headed towards the nice looking house.

"Y'all niggaz hurry up," Kim said as she pulled her 9mm from out of her purse and hopped out the back seat and got behind the wheel.

Inside the house, Capo and Moose trashed the place until Moose found a duffle bag hiding in the stove. "Jackpot," he yelled as he smiled when he felt how heavy the duffle bag was.

"What's in that bitch?" Capo asked sticking his gun back in his waistband. Moose opened up the bag and found that it was filled with money and guns. "Guess they won't need these anymore," Moose said as he and Capo walked right back out the front door as if they owned the place. Once they were inside the car, Kim quickly pulled off.

\*\*\*

Angela strolled down the street looking for the perfect vehicle for her next mission. A blonde wig and dark shades hide her identity. She walked up on a 1999 Ford Explorer and a smirk danced on her lips.

# THE TEFLON QUEEN

Angela quickly elbowed the glass, shattering it into pieces as she stuck her arm inside and let herself in. Once inside, Angela jammed a pocketknife in the ignition and made the truck come to life. She pulled off to go handle her business. Angela drove in complete silence as she thought about the best way to take out her target. As she continued to drive, she began to think about James. *"I wonder what he's doing right now,"* she thought out loud, as she pulled his card from out of her pocket and dialed his number. On the fifth ring, he finally answered.

"Hello?"

"Can I speak to James please?" Angela asked politely in her schoolgirl voice.

"Who is this?" James asked not recognizing the out of town number.

"Angie," Angela replied. "Damn how many women you got calling you?"

"Stop it," James laughed. "It's about time you called. I thought you had forgotten about me for a second."

"Had to let you sweat it out for minute," Angela chuckled. She loved how smooth and calm James voice sounded over the phone. "Is this supposed to be your sexy voice?"

"There you go," James laughed. "What you getting into tonight?"

"Nothing much," Angela replied. "Just have to take care of some business real quick. I should be done in about thirty minutes. What you got planned for the night?"

"Getting dressed and about to go to the club," James told her.

"Oh so I see you are a real party animal," Angela said half-jokingly, as she pulled up three blocks away from Sammy's house.

"Work related," James replied. "I should be done around 3 am and if that's not too late I would like to see you."

"What we going to do at three o'clock in the morning?" Angela asked as she climbed into the back seat and removed her Barrett M107 .50 caliber sniper rifle.

"Maybe I can cook for you," James suggested. "What you like to eat?"

"Surprise me," Angela said loading a round into the chamber.

"So it's a date?"

"Yeah text me your address and I'll be there around 3:30," Angela said ending the call. Once she hung up the phone, she focused on Sammy's house. As Angela waited for Sammy to show his face, she thought about going to see James later on that night. She hadn't been with a man in so long due to how she made her money. Angela felt butterflies in her stomach. Angela laughed as she felt herself feeling like she was in high school again. After sitting in the back seat for four and a half hours, Sammy finally stepped out his house surrounded by plenty of security. "About time," Angela whispered as she aimed her rifle at Sammy. Once Sammy's head was in the middle of the crosshair, Angela pulled the trigger shooting through the back window of the Explorer. Sammy and his crew headed towards the vehicle that waited curbside until Sammy's body dropped out of the blue. Immediately, Sammy's security drew their weapons and scrambled to find out where the shot came from. Once Angela saw Sammy's body drop, she broke down her rifle, hopped back behind the wheel, and peeled off undetected.

\*\*\*

# THE TEFLON QUEEN

Capo took a swig from his bottle of RosayRosay as he sat back in the booth at his own lounge. He watched, as everyone in the lounge enjoyed themselves and partied like there was no tomorrow.

"You a'ight?" Bone asked as he took a seat next to Capo. He knew something was wrong with him because the place was full of beautiful women and Capo was just sitting over in the corner all by himself.

"Yeah... I'm just chilling," Capo said, forcing a smile on his face.

"What's on your mind fam?" Bone pressed. Before Capo could even respond, two white detectives entered his booth and helped themselves to a seat.

"What's up Capo?" The taller detective asked calling Capo by his street name just to mess with him.

"Fuck y'all want?" Capo asked in an uninterested tone. "Y'all ain't got nothing else better to do?"

"Your name was brought up in a shooting that went down earlier today," the shorter detective said speaking for the first time. "Care to tell us about that?"

"Am I under arrest or what?" Capo asked as if the detectives were becoming an annoyance. "That's what I thought," he said as he and Bone got up and posted up over by the bar. "I'm tired of these motherfuckers!" Capo huffed. Ever since he and Wayne had went their separate ways, Capo noticed that more and more heat had been coming down on him and his crew. "If it's not one thing it's another," Capo said taking another swig from his bottle of Rosay.

A loud commotion at the front entrance caused Capo and Bone to turn their attention to the front door. A man wearing about four chains around his neck, an iced out bracelet and watch, argued at the door with one of the bouncers. After the two went back and forth for a few minutes, the man and his entourage were finally allowed to enter. The mystery man demanded the entire lounge's attention as he bopped towards the bar.

"Who is this clown?" Capo asked unimpressed.

"Some nigga named Crazy Moe," Bone answered.

"Oh that's Crazy Moe?" Capo said as he walked over towards the man and his entourage, but was immediately stopped by one of Crazy Moe's goons.

"Can I help you?" the goon asked with his face crumbled up looking Capo up and down.

"I need to have a word with Moe," Capo said as he took a sip from his bottle.

"Nah," the goon said shaking his head. "Crazy Moe came here to party, not talk to no clowns."

Capo sighed loudly as he stole on the goon dropping him with one punch. Once the bouncers in the club saw Capo swing on the man, they quickly ran up to the scene to make sure no harm was done to their boss. The rest of Crazy Moe's goons stood face to face with Capo, Bone, and the bouncers.

"What's the problem?" Crazy Moe asked stepping to the front of the line with a champagne glass in his hand.

"I need to talk to you over here for a second," Capo said as he and Crazy Moe stepped over to the side. "What up?" Crazy Moe asked sipping from his glass.

"Listen fam," Capo began. "I don't know who you are and honestly I don't care. I'm only going to tell you this once," he said looking Crazy Moe in his eyes. "Stay the fuck off my corners! Next nigga I see on any of my corners who claim to work for you, I'm coming to see you personally!"

Crazy Moe smiled and took another sip from his drink before he replied. "I don't know if you heard or not, but I work for Wayne now and I have full permission to post up on any block I choose to; understand?" Crazy Moe smiled. "I took your old spot so that makes me the new boss of the streets now."

"Is that right?" Capo asked as he clutched his Rosay bottle even tighter in his hand. He so badly wanted to bust the bottle over Crazy Moe's head, but he knew that would start an all-out war out in the streets between him and Wayne, and right now wasn't a good time for Capo to be in the middle of a street war. "Me and Wayne have a personal agreement to stay the fuck out of each other's way so I'm telling you straight up, I don't like you," Capo paused. "So please stay the fuck out my way!"

"You got it chump... I mean champ," Crazy Moe said with a smirk as he broke out in a two-step as the lounge got hype when Soulja Boy's song "Pretty Boy Swag" came blasting through the speakers. Capo so badly wanted to set it off in the lounge, but since Crazy Moe now worked for Wayne, there wasn't much Capo could do, but just hope Crazy Moe didn't cross the line. Just as Capo was about to head back over to his booth, a caramel complexion girl grabbed his hand. "You not going nowhere until you dance with me," the woman told Capo rather then ask him. She threw her ass up against Capo's penis as the two grinded together to the beat. Capo grabbed the woman's waist as she bent all the way over touching the floor. After three straight songs, Capo was tired.

"Where are you going?" the woman asked. "I know you not tired already?"

"Yeah Imma go sit down for a while. I'll be right back," Capo lied. The real reason he didn't want to dance no more was because the .45 in his waistband threatened to fall out because of how wild the woman was dancing. Besides Capo didn't like to get all sweaty unless he was having sex. *"Fuck this shit! I'm going home,"* Capo said to himself as he exited the lounge. When Capo made it outside, Bone quickly caught up to him. "Where you headed?"

"Going home," Capo answered. Usually Capo was the last one to turn it in for the night, but tonight was just one of those nights where all he wanted to do was go home and relax.

"I feel you," Bone agreed as the two walked through the parking lot until a voice stopped them.

"A, yo my man," the voice called out. When Capo and Bone turned around, they saw a well-built gentleman coming towards them.

"You know this fool?" Capo asked.

"Never seen this nigga a day in my life," Bone replied as the big man walked up.

"A, yo my man," the well-built man said looking at Capo. "You know that girl you was dancing with back there? That was my wife!" the man huffed making all kind of hand gestures while he spoke.

"Oh, you talking about that whack ass bitch I was dancing with?" Capo said purposely trying to get a reaction out of the man so he could have a reason to wash him up.

"Yo dog watch how you talk about my wife!" the stranger said taking a step forward. Without thinking twice, Capo quickly punched the man in his mouth sending him stumbling backwards. Before Capo even got a chance to swing again, Bone had already sent a bullet into the man's stomach.

# THE TEFLON QUEEN

"Fuck!" Capo cursed as he and Bone hopped in his Benz and peeled off leaving the big man lying in the parking lot leaking.

"Fuck!" Capo cursed again looking through his rearview mirror. He knew Bone shooting that man was only going to bring more heat to his lounge. "Bone listen to me," Capo said as he weaved in and out of the highway traffic. "You can't keep popping off like that!"

"Fuck you expect me to do?" Bone asked looking at Capo as if he was crazy. "I saw you swing on the nigga so I made my move." Capo was about to say something else, but he knew he would just be wasting his time. Cats like Bone, all they cared about were their name and the more work they put in, the more famous their name became on the streets. "Imma holla at you tomorrow," Capo said as he dropped Bone off at his crib then headed home himself. When Capo walked inside his house, he immediately noticed a noise coming from upstairs. "What the fuck?" Capo said to himself as he pulled out his .45 and slowly and cautiously made his way up the steps. When he entered his room, he slowly lowered his gun when he saw Kim lying across his bed butt naked.

"You were going to shoot me Daddy?" Kim said in a seductive tone.

"Never," Capo replied as he removed his shirt and sat down on the bed.

Kim looked over at him as if he was crazy. "Pants too," she told him.

Capo removed his pants, flopped down on the bed, and exhaled loudly.

"What's the matter baby?" Kim asked.

"Nothing baby," Capo replied looking up at the ceiling.

# SILK WHITE

"I know just what you need to make you feel better," Kim said as she pulled Capo's dick out through the hole in his boxers and gave him just what he needed.

*\*\**

Angela arrived on James' block and she immediately circled the block twice before pulling her Lambo inside James' driveway. She double-checked her appearance in the rearview mirror, her butterfly doors opened, and she stepped out the vehicle. Angela wore a red Marc Jacobs dress to match with her red lipstick and the expensive red four-inch pumps that adorned her feet. Angela walked up to front door and rung the bell as she nervously waited for an answer. Seconds later, James answered the door with a white apron over his clothes.

"What's good ma?" James asked as he stepped to the side and watched Angela enter his home. His house was kind of small but Angela didn't mind. She wasn't there to see his house. She was there to see him. "Something smells good," Angela said, helping herself to a seat at the bar like counter.

"I'm making my special dish," James smiled. "Steak, mash potatoes, and broccoli."

"Sounds good to me," Angela said as she looked around. James walked over and poured Angela a glass of red wine. "Make yourself at home," he said as he walked over to his entertainment system and threw Trey Songz' C.D. in the player at a medium volume. James then helped himself to a seat next to Angela. "Thanks for coming," he said looking in her eyes.

"What are you thanking me for?" Angela smiled.

"For spending time with a federal agent," James said as the two enjoyed a laugh.

"You ain't too bad for a cop," Angela said pouring herself another glass of wine. For the rest of the night Angela and James sat talking and getting to know each other better. She found out that just because James worked for the F.E.D.S didn't mean he was a bad person. He was actually just doing his job and Angela had to respect that. She just prayed that if one day if he ever found out what she did for a living, he would respect it.

"So what made you want to become an agent?" Angela asked as she lay in James arms on the couch while the two continued to get their sip on.

"Ever since I was a kid, I always wanted to capture big criminals even when I used to play cops and robbers with my friends. I made sure I was always the cop."

"So you know any special techniques?" Angela asked.

"Every technique there is," James told her meaning every word. Truth be told James Carter took his job very serious and he always got his man.

"Are you a good shooter?"

"The best!" James boasted. "I'm a sharp shooter. I graduated the top shooter in my class."

"Damn!" Angela said pretending to be impressed. "I guess I better stay on your good side," she joked.

"I would never hurt you," James told her and for some reason Angela believed him. For the rest of the night, the two talked until they fell asleep in each other's arms on the couch.

# CHAPTER 9

Wayne sat in his office reading the daily newspaper when he looked up and saw Crazy Moe and two other men enter his office. "What's good boss man?" Crazy Moe said giving Wayne some dap.

"Who these two niggaz?" Wayne asked sitting his paper down.

"These the two grimiest stickup kids I could find for you," Crazy Moe replied.

"Good," Wayne said looking at the two-stickup kids. "I hope y'all ready to put in some work!"

"This is what we do," Cash, the leader out of the two confirmed. He and his partner Dough Boy, were the toughest and meanest stickup kids in New York. When they came, they always came correct. When Cash and Dough Boy went on a job, there was no such thing as a smooth job. Wherever they went, a blood trail always followed.

"Who you want us to rob anyway?" Dough Boy asked. He got that name because he looked like Ice Cube when he played in the movie "Boyz in the Hood."

"Capo," Wayne answered. He didn't like how Capo was going around acting as if he was the one running things so now Wayne was going to show him who the real boss was. "I want y'all to just to rob him and that's it. Don't kill him. I just want to teach him a little lesson that's all."

"How much is this job paying?" Cash asked greedily rubbing his hands together.

"$15,000.00" Wayne answered. "And make sure it's done in public. I want the streets to be talking about this one," he said as he slid Cash an envelope full of bills.

"Not a problem," Cash said as he and Dough Boy got up and left.

"Damn you must really hate Capo," Crazy Moe said helping himself to a seat.

"I don't hate him. I just have to teach him a lesson that's all," Wayne said fixing himself a drink. "But fuck all that! I need you to go downtown and put up that order of guns I just brought from that Chinese motherfucker."

"I got you," Crazy Moe said as he left Wayne alone in his office. Wayne felt bad for what he was doing, but he had to let the streets know that he was still the boss.

***

Shekia stepped inside Capo's office in the back of the lounge and saw Capo with Bone chilling and having a few drinks. "What's up y'all?" Shekia asked.

Now that she had been hanging around the crew, she saw for herself that they were just like everyone else. All they were doing was their jobs, but whether it was right or wrong was a different story. Still Shekia didn't judge them. The whole crew was cool and she got along with everybody except for Kim.

"Come sit down and have a drink," Capo said handing her a bottle of Grey Goose. Shekia gladly accepted the bottle as she helped herself to a seat and poured herself a strong drink. "What y'all doing just chilling?"

"Yeah, we are about to take a ride. I think you should come with us," Bone suggested.

"Where y'all going?" Shekia asked curiously.

"It's a surprise," Bone said as he stood up with a smile on his face.

Capo looked over at Shekia. "Don't feel bad. He wouldn't tell me either."

Shekia shrugged her shoulders. "I'm down," she said especially since she didn't have anything else to do for the rest of the night. When the trio stepped outside they hopped in Bone's cocaine-white Lexus. "Just sit back and enjoy the ride," Bone smiled as he pulled out of the parking spot and out into traffic. Forty-five minutes later Bone pulled up in front of a mansion.

"What's this?" Capo asked with a smile on his face.

"Me, Kim, and Moose rented out this mansion," Bone told him. "Tonight we partying!" As the trio walked up, they saw people everywhere. There were people on the front lawn, out in the back, and the music was blasting so loud one could hear it before you even reached the front door.

"This how we party around here," Capo told Shekia as they entered the mansion. Inside there were butt naked women everywhere. People were laying around sniffing coke, smoking weed, and getting drunk.

"Triffling," Shekia whispered as she walked past a couple having sex right on the steps out in the open. Capo walked over to the kitchen area and grabbed a bottle of RosayRosay from off the counter. Everybody who was everybody was at the party, from drug dealers to strippers to gold-diggers.

"The real party is out here!" Moose yelled when he spotted Bone and Capo. When the trio made it out in the back yard there had to be at least 800 people out by the pool area partying. "Heeeeyy baby," Kim yelled walking up dripping wet in her bra and panties as she hugged Capo getting him all wet.

"What's good," Capo replied looking at all the naked women in the pool.

"Who all these other niggaz?"

"I don't know. We just wanted to throw you a nice big party since we've noticed you been a little down lately," Kim answered.

"Yo ma, you coming back in the water?" A butt naked dripping wet man interrupted asking Kim.

"Yo don't you see me over here talking?" Kim huffed. "Fuck outta here," she said waving off him.

"Don't get mad at him," Capo said with a hint of jealousy in his voice.

"Go finish talking to your boyfriend."

"Yeah I think Imma go do that cause I see you brought your lil girlfriend," Kim said looking Shekia up and down before she sucked her teeth and went back and hopped in the pool.

"Y'all two needs to stop playing already and make it official. Everybody knows y'all in love," Bone said shaking his head as he undressed down to his boxers, hopped in the pool and quickly engaged in a conversation with a butt naked female.

**SILK WHITE**

"Sorry about that," Capo apologized to Shekia as he began to undress down to his boxers. He stuck his gun in the pocket of his jeans. "I'm about to hop in this pool with all these hoes," he said. "It's naked and half naked men all over this motherfucker so get in where you fit in," Capo said as he walked over to the pool and slowly slid in the water with all his jewelry on and his bottle of RosayRosay in hand. Before Capo was even all the way in the water, a diesel gentleman who looked like he had been working out since he was born approached Shekia.

"What's good ma?" The strong man asked cupping Shekia's ass. "You wanna get in the water with me?"

"Excuse me?" Shekia said pushing the man off of her.

"I said do you want to get in the water with me," the diesel guy repeated.

"No thank you," Shekia replied as she walked away and took a seat on one of the beach chairs that surrounded the pool area. *"This some crazy shit,"* Shekia said to herself as she watched people having sex with strangers and getting high right in the open. She was finally starting to realize that with money, there isn't much one couldn't do.

As Shekia laid on the beach chair bobbing her head to music, she noticed two men over in the corner looking like they were up to no good. From the look on their faces, Shekia knew that something bad was about to go down. She quickly got up from her seat and went over towards the edge of the pool.

"Capo!" she called out, but Capo was too busy being entertained by two naked Spanish women. "Capo!" she yelled again. Just as she got ready to call his name again, the diesel man who had grabbed her ass pulled her down into the water.

"What's up baby you was calling me?" he smiled as he locked her in a bear hug and began dunking her in the water.

# THE TEFLON QUEEN

"Yo chill!" Shekia screamed as the strong man dunked her under the water again. Once Shekia got out of the big man's grip, she quickly turned and smacked the shit out of him.

"Yeah baby that rough shit turns me on!" The diesel man said loudly.

It was obvious he was coked-up out of his mind. When Shekia looked back, she saw Capo all the way at the other end of the pool. "Fuck!" she cursed.

The pool was so packed that she couldn't swim over to where he was. All she could do was squeeze through all the naked partygoers as they enjoyed themselves and splashed water all over the place.

\*\*\*

Cash and Dough Boy sat over on the other side of the pool scheming.

"Look at these fools," Dough Boy said in a disgusted manner. "All that money and this is what they do with it."

"Don't worry, we're going to get you everything you need," Cash assured his best friend. The two men had been there for over four hours waiting for the perfect time to make their move. From the look on Dough Boy's face, Cash could tell he was sick and tired of waiting.

"Imma go lock the door. Once I do that, it's on," Cash told Dough Boy as he got up and walked over to the door that separated the backyard from the house. Once Cash made sure the door was locked, he gave Dough Boy the go-ahead nod. Dough Boy saw a group of naked women and men standing in front of him by the pool. He quickly pulled out his Uzi and fired into the crowd sending bodies flying into the water. Once the gunfire erupted throughout the backyard, everybody started going crazy trying to escape. Dough Boy fired his Uzi into another crowd before he had everyone's attention.

"Everybody calm down," Cash announced as he pulled his .40 cal from his waistband and walked straight over to the edge of the pool where Capo stood in the water. "This your party?"

"You better kill me now," Capo said taking a swig from his bottle, as he looked Cash in the eye. A smirk danced on Cash's lips. He liked how tough Capo thought he was.

"Get out the pool," he said in a calm voice as he watched Capo do as he was told. "Get rid of that bottle," Cash told him as he watched Capo toss the bottle of Rosay in the water.

Cash looked and saw that Capo wore about three chains around his neck. One chain was a capital "C" made out of diamonds. "Gimme all that shit!" Cash barked as he removed the chains from around Capo's neck and placed them on his own neck. "What that "C" stand for?" Cash asked admiring the chain.

"It stands for Capo," Capo replied coldly.

"Well now it stands for Cash motherfucker!" Cash smiled as he hit Capo across the face with his gun sending him splashing into the water.

While he was humiliating Capo, Dough Boy took all the money out of all the pants and purses he saw laying around. When he was all done, he had a garbage bag full of cash and wallets.

"The rest of you motherfuckers better not try to be a hero," Cash said as he saw one of Capo's goons looking at him as if he was ready to kill him. "Fuck is you looking at?" Cash huffed as he shot the man in the face, causing women who stood next to the man to scream.

# THE TEFLON QUEEN

"We got everything?" Cash asked looking over at Dough Boy. Dough Boy nodded his head as the two men quickly hopped over the fence and ran towards the getaway car that they had waiting for them. Once they were gone, all hell broke loose.

"Find out who the two niggaz were," Capo said washing the blood from his face with the pool water before he got out the pool. Immediately, all that could be heard was screeching tires as two cars full of goons drove around hoping to catch the two men before they got too far.

"Fuck!" Capo cursed mad that he had been caught slipping.

"I was trying to warn you," Shekia said looking at Capo's wound.

"What? You know them niggaz or something?" Capo asked.

"No, I don't know them," Shekia answered quickly. "I saw them over there scheming!"

"So why the fuck you ain't say nothing?" Bone asked jumping into the conversation.

"I tried to, but he stopped me," Shekia said pointing to the diesel guy who was now putting his jeans back on.

"Who this nigga right here," Capo said pointing at the diesel guy.

"Yeah him," Shekia responded as she looked on. Capo walked up to the big man and grilled him. "You know them niggaz?"

"Nah I don't know them," the big man said throwing his hands up in surrender. "I just came here to get my party on."

"So why was you stopping my home girl from getting to me?"

SILK WHITE

"I...I...I thought she wanted to party. All I was trying to do was hit that," the big man said honestly. He didn't want no trouble, but from the looks of things he was about to have a long night.

"So, if she would have got the message to me none of this would have happened. So this means this is all your fault," Capo said as he saw Moose creeping up on the big man from behind with a wooden baseball bat in his hands.

"No, Capo I swear I didn't know what was about to go down," the big man pleaded. "All I was trying to do..." the baseball bat connecting with the back of his head ended the conversation as everybody looked on as the big man's face smacked the concrete. Moose continued to swing the bat with all his might.

"You...wanna...set...motherfuckers...up!" he growled as he beat the big man until he no longer existed. Moose spit on the man's body as he dropped the baseball bat and walked off.

Shekia couldn't believe what she just witnessed. If she knew they were going to kill the man, she wouldn't have said anything. She just watched as a few of Capo's goons picked the big man's body up and tossed him in the pool with the rest of the dead bodies.

"Come on we gotta go before the cops get here," Capo said as he grabbed Shekia's arm and rushed her through the house towards the exit.

"Moose do me a favor and take her home for me," Capo said handing Shekia off to Moose.

"You have to go to the hospital," Kim said looking at the cut on the side of Capo's eye.

"Fuck a hospital," Capo huffed. He was embarrassed that he had been robbed in front of all of his peers. He knew news like this was going

73

to spread through the hood quickly, meaning he had to find the two men who had robbed him even quicker.

"What you need me to do?" Bone asked ready to put in some work.

"Nothing," Capo replied. "Imma go home and get some rest. By the time I wake up, we should know exactly who these clowns are and where to find them," Capo said as he and Kim hopped in her Audi and peeled off.

\*\*\*

"That shit went easier than I expected," Cash said as he pulled the stolen Acura up in front of Dough Boy's house.

"What was that shit back there about?" Dough Boy asked as he began counting what they had collected for the night.

"Nothing," Cash replied with a smile. He knew Capo thought he was untouchable and he wanted to show him that anybody could be touched. "How much we got other there?"

"Broke ass niggaz," Dough Boy huffed. "$16,000.00," he said handing Cash half of the money.

"Nah," Cash said not accepting the money. "Keep that. We going to get you everything you need," he paused. "You like my brother so your problems are my problems."

Dough Boy let Cash's word sink in before replying. "Good looking out. I appreciate that. Imma make sure I give all the money I borrowed from you back to you."

"Dont worry about it. It's nothing," Cash said as he gave Dough Boy dap, watched him exit the car and head into the house. Once Cash was sure Dough Boy was inside safely, he pulled off. He knew his partner was going through some tough times in his life and he planned to do whatever he could to help.

Dough Boy stepped inside his house and saw his wife Monica sitting on the couch in the dark.

"You alright baby?" Dough Boy asked as he cut the lights on. From where he was standing, he could see that Monica was crying. "How's he doing?" Dough Boy asked as he sat next to her and looked down at the floor.

"It's getting worse," Monica told him in between sobs. "We have to get him some help."

"Where is he?" Dough Boy asked standing to his feet.

"In his room," Monica replied as she tried to wipe her tears away.

Dough Boy walked in the back of the house to his son's room. He took a deep breath before he entered. When he stepped inside, he saw his son Lil Dough lying in his bed sound asleep. As Dough Boy got closer to the bed, he saw that Lil Dough was sweating like crazy. *"Damn!"* he mumbled as a single tear escaped from his eye. His son Lil Dough needed a heart transplant. His heart was no longer able to pump blood all throughout the young man's body and the doctor told Dough Boy that his son was suffering from heart failure. Dough Boy stood over his son and just looked as sweat covered the boy's whole face. His skin even began to darken. A tear fell from Dough Boy's eye as he watched his son's chest heave up and down desperately sucking in air. "Imma get you taken care of, just hang in there," Dough Boy whispered as he sat in the empty chair that sat beside Lil Dough's bed and watched him sleep like he did every night.

\*\*\*

# THE TEFLON QUEEN

Shekia walked in her house trying to make the least bit of noise she possibly could. She didn't want her mother to wake up and talk her ears off. That was the last thing she needed right now. Just as Shekia passed the living room, the lights shot on.

"What the hell happened to you?" Ms. Pat said standing next to the light switch with her hands on her hips. "Why the hell are your clothes wet," she asked. "And is that blood on your shirt?"

"Mommy now is not the time," Shekia said, waving her mother off as she headed in her room. She didn't want to hear her shit tonight. All Shekia wanted to do was take a nice hot shower.

"You were out hanging with those drug dealers again weren't you?" Ms. Pat said busting in Shekia's room. "I'm telling you," she said pointing her finger at her daughter. "Those animals don't give a shit about you. When are you going to realize that?"

"Mommy please leave me alone," Shekia huffed as she removed her wet clothes.

"I'm not going to leave you alone," Ms. Pat continued her rant. "Why is there blood on your clothes? And why are you all wet?"

"Mommy I'm grown and I can handle myself, alright?" Shekia yelled louder than she meant to do.

"This how you talk to your mother now?" Ms. Pat said looking Shekia up and down. "Those animals are changing you already. You don't want me to bother you anymore; then fine I won't, but don't come running back here when those animals leave you for dead!" Ms. Pat said as she stormed out of Shekia's room and slammed the door behind her.

Shekia hated to have to talk to her mother like that, but she knew no matter how she explained the situation, Ms. Pat just wouldn't understand.

# SILK WHITE

When Shekia got out the shower, she quickly dried off and flopped down on her bed butt naked as she stared up at the ceiling as replays of what happened at the party ran through her mind. Her cell phone ringing snapped her out of her thoughts as she answered the phone without even looking at the caller I.D. "Hello?"

"What's up?" the voice on the other end replied. Shekia immediately recognized the voice. It was Scarface.

"Don't you be what's uping me," she said as if she had an attitude.

"What's wrong baby?" Scarface chuckled.

"What? I thought you forgot how to use a phone for a minute" Shekia huffed.

"My bad baby I just been a little busy on my end, but what's good? I want to see you. That's why I'm calling you," Scarface told her.

"I don't know if I wanna see you right now," Shekia said trying to play hardball since she had the ball in her court.

"Come on baby I'm serious," Scarface said. He knew she wanted to see him just as bad as he wanted and needed to see her.

"When you want to see me?" Shekia asked playing with her nipples.

"Tonight!" Scarface replied.

"I'm not scheduled to make another trip out there until next week," Shekia said wishing she could have gone and spent time with him tonight.

# THE TEFLON QUEEN

"Fuck that! Get dress right now," Scarface said. "One of my peoples is in front of your house right now. Get dressed and he's going to take you to the airport and you can go back next week when it's time for you to make the drop-off."

"Are you serious?" Shekia asked shocked.

"My man is waiting right outside for you. Go look out your window," Scarface said in a smooth tone. Shekia got up, walked over to her window, and peeked out the blinds. Outside she saw a black Lexus parked right out front with the lights on.

"How did you know where I live?" Shekia asked curiously.

"I did my homework on you Ms. Shekia," Scarface laughed. "Now hurry up and get dressed. You don't have to bring nothing with you, but what you got on your back."

Shekia thought about it for a second. *"Fuck it,"* she told herself. She didn't have anything else to do so she figured why not. "I'm getting dressed now," she said before hanging up the phone.

# CHAPTER 10

Capo sat parked in his Benz as he waited for Bone to meet him at this location. He filled up his foam cup with more liquor as he continued to wait for Bone to arrive. All Capo could think about was getting his hands on the man who had robbed him and humiliated him. *"I'mma do that nigga dirty when I catch him,"* Capo said to himself as he took another sip from his cup. About ten minutes later Capo saw Bone bopping down the street with his Yankee hat pulled down low.

"What's good five?" Bone asked as he hopped in the passenger seat and gave Capo dap.

"What's the word?" Capo asked getting straight to the point.

"A'ight" Bone began. "The nigga that robbed you name is Cash, and his partner's name is Dough Boy. Word on the streets is these two niggaz been sticking motherfuckers up for years, but you want to hear what's even crazier?" Bone paused. "They supposed to be real tight with ya boy Crazy Moe."

"And Crazy Moe works for Wayne," Capo said out loud.

"Bingo!" Bone said excitedly. "That nigga has been behind this shit the whole time."

"That bitch ass nigga," Capo said out loud. He knew Wayne was upset that he had went and did his own thing, but he didn't think the man would ever try to do anything to hurt him. At least that's what Capo thought. "Fuck that! We bringing it to that bitch ass nigga Wayne!"

"It's about time," Bone smiled. "I heard this clown Crazy Moe is at Satin every other night. You wanna ride up there and see if we see that clown?" Before Bone could even finish his sentence, Capo had already started up the car and pulled off.

***

"Good looking on that lick you put me on to the other day," Cash said as he gave Crazy Moe a pound. The two men sat in Crazy Moe's Range Rover in the parking lot right outside the club.

"Don't mention it," Crazy Moe replied. "But fuck all that robbery shit. When you gon come and be down on my team?" He needed a good leader like Cash on his team and was willing to pay top dollar to recruit him.

"Nah selling drugs ain't really my thing. It takes too much time and it ain't worth the risk," Cash said taking two pulls from his blunt before passing it to Crazy Moe.

"You ain't gotta sell shit. All I need you to do is keep motherfuckers in line," Crazy Moe said trying to make the job seem easier than it really was. "Plus once you on Wayne's team, you become connected," Crazy Moe said, pulling three large stacks of money from his pocket to show Cash it wasn't a game.

"I mean that's cool and all, but I'mma just stick to what I know," Cash said as he pulled out his cell phone and sent a quick text message.

"Anyway," Crazy Moe said trying from another angle. "Wayne wants to see you."

"For what?" Cash asked taking the blunt back.

"He heard about the good ass job you did the other night and wants to holla at you," Crazy Moe replied.

# SILK WHITE

"Tell Wayne I have nothing to say to him unless he needs me to rob somebody for him. If not, then we don't have anything to talk about. You dig?" Cash asked in a neutral tone.

"A'ight I'll tell him," Crazy Moe said as he watched Cash hop out his Range Rover and into his Acura with heavy tints.

"Stupid motherfucker," he said once Cash had driven off. Crazy Moe sat in his Range Rover until he finished the blunt he was smoking on. "Fuck that! It's party time," he said as he hopped out the Range Rover.

As soon as Crazy Moe's feet touched the concrete, he felt the barrel of a gun pressed to the back of his head. "Don't try to be no hero!" The gunman said in a calm voice as he slowly removed the chains from around Crazy Moe's neck. "What else you got on you?" he said tapping Crazy Moe's pockets and then taking all the cash he had on him. "Better me then the IRS nigga," the gunman said as he hit Crazy Moe in the back of the head with his gun knocking him unconscious. Once the gunman was sure Crazy Moe was out cold, he quickly ran and hopped in the passenger side of the Acura as it pulled off.

\*\*\*

"This the club right here?" Capo asked as he slowly pulled into the club's parking lot.

"Yeah this is the right club," Bone told him as the two cruised through the parking lot looking for a place to park. "Yo ain't that bitch ass nigga right there?" Capo said pointing. He saw Crazy Moe standing in the middle of the parking lot surrounded by goons. "I'mma drive by real slow. I want you to hit as many of them motherfuckers as you can!"

Bone nodded his head as he pulled out his .9mm and cocked it back. As Capo cruised by, Bone hung out the window and opened fire.

# THE TEFLON QUEEN

POW! POW! POW! POW! POW! POW! was all that could be heard followed by screeching tires.

When Crazy Moe heard the gunshots, he quickly dropped down to the ground not wanting to get his head blown off. Once the shots finished ringing out, two dead bodies laid on top of him. "Yo Moe you alright?" he heard one of his goons asking in a high pitched voice.

"I'm good," Crazy Moe replied as he got up and hopped in his Range Rover and burnt rubber. "Fuck!" Crazy Moe cursed loudly as he banged the steering wheel with his hand. Not only had he been shot, but he also got robbed all in the same night. *"Whoever did this shit is going to pay,"* he said to himself as he heard his cell phone ringing.

"Hello!" he answered.

"Oh did I catch you at a bad time," the voice on the other end asked. As soon as Crazy Moe heard the woman's voice on the other end, he immediately calmed down. "No you didn't catch me at a bad time. Why, what's up?" he asked.

"Oh I was just in your neighborhood and I thought I might drop by if that's okay with you?" the woman said.

"Sure that's fine. How long is it going to take for you to get there?" Crazy Moe asked.

"About five minutes."

"I'll be there in ten so just wait for me okay?"

"No problem," the woman said before she hung up. Crazy Moe put the pedal to the medal as he rushed home. He was excited to see this woman and he knew if he didn't see her tonight, there was no telling when he would see her again. Crazy Moe pulled up in front of his house and saw a cherry red Lamborghini parked in his driveway. He pulled up right behind the car as he saw the owner of the car sitting on the hood looking as beautiful as ever. "Hey what's up? I didn't have you waiting long did I?" Crazy Moe asked as he walked up to the woman.

"Oh my God James! Are you alright?" Angela said when she saw James clothes covered in blood. "Did you get shot?"

"No, it's not my blood," James told her as they stepped inside.

"What happened to you?" Angela asked with her voice full of concern.

"I'm working undercover," James said as he slipped out of his bloody clothes.

"Oh my God! The back of your head is bleeding," Angela said as she went to the bathroom and returned carrying a wet rag. "Come here," she said as James sat down in between her legs on the floor. Angela was trained to heal any kind of wounds. She quickly pulled her emergency medical kit from out of her purse and began to stitch up the back of James head. James sat on the floor quietly in his draws as Angela stitched him up.

"Okay so you want to tell me what happened?" Angela asked.

"I got robbed and shot at all in the same night," James laughed. "I can't wait to arrest these guys."

"This sounds like a serious case," Angela said hoping James would tell her a little bit more about the case. "You almost got killed tonight? You don't think it might be time to leave this case alone?"

"I can't," James said quickly. "I'm so close to taking this fucker down to just quit right now. In a few weeks this will all be over."

# THE TEFLON QUEEN

"So what is it like being undercover?" Angela asked as she continued to stitch up the back of James head.

"It's crazy," James replied. "But I love the challenge," he admitted.

"All done," Angela said once she finished stitching him up. Angela hated the fact that James was a federal agent, but at the same time, she didn't want to see him get hurt. She knew how rough it could be in the game and she just hoped James knew what he was doing because if he didn't, he wouldn't be around for much longer.

"I'mma go hop in the shower real quick. Make yourself at home," James said as he disappeared in the bathroom. Angela walked over to the kitchen area and helped herself to a glass of wine as she waited for James to get out of the shower. As Angela sat sipping on her glass of wine, she saw James' weapon lying in his holster strapped to the belt on his jeans. She walked over and grabbed the pistol; a government issued .45 acp handgun. She smiled as she placed his gun back in the holster. Minutes later, James came out the bathroom with just a towel wrapped around his waist.

"Your body ain't too bad," Angela said checking out James's six-pack.

"You know I have to stay in shape," James chuckled as he picked up his bloody clothes from off the floor and then disappeared in his bedroom. Angela quickly followed him into the room and closed the door behind her. Before James had a chance to say anything, Angela stuck her tongue in his mouth as the two began kissing like animals. Angela dropped her glass on the floor as she removed James towel from around his waist. As soon as the towel hit the floor, she started to work him into stiffness with her hand. James ripped Angela's blouse open as he shoved one of her perfect sized breast in his mouth while he watched Angela wiggle out of the skirt she wore. Underneath her skirt, she only wore a silk gold thong. James effortlessly ripped her thong off so that

SILK WHITE

she stood before him butt naked. James scooped Angela up in the air so that his face was face to face with her nicely trimmed pussy.

"Oh my God," Angela moaned as she wrapped her legs around James' neck when she felt his tongue massaging her clit. James held Angela up in the air as he sucked and licked her pussy as if it was the last pussy he would ever see again in his life.

"Oh I'm about to cum," Angela announced loving every minute of the pleasure she was receiving. James quickly lifted Angela up and hung her upside down as he continued to tongue kiss her clit with passion. As Angela hung upside down, she grabbed a hold of James's dick, put it in her mouth, and started to suck the shit out of it. She moaned as she worked her hands and mouth at the same time. When James felt himself about to cum he gently laid Angela on the bed as he watched her climb in the doggy style position.

"Damn," James groaned as he felt Angela's walls wrapped around his dick like a glove. From the tightness of Angela's pussy James could tell that she hadn't been fucked in a while. James stuck his finger in Angela's mouth as he sped up his strokes. Just as James was about to cum, he quickly pulled out and exploded all over Angela's ass. "Damn!" James huffed, breathing heavy as he flopped down on the bed. Angela just lay across the bed naked for a few seconds to get her thoughts together. She hadn't cum like that in a long time and she just needed a second to catch her breath. James got up and went to the bathroom and when he returned he was carrying a wet rag as he cleaned Angela up and then laid down next to her where the two fell asleep in each other's arms.

\*\*\*

Capo stepped out of his crib and looked over both shoulders as he walked up to his new all-white, bulletproof B.M.W. Capo recklessly pulled away from the curb blasting Yo Gotti's new mixtape. Once Capo learned that Wayne had tried to get him robbed and killed, he knew that he could no longer trust anybody so from now on he decided to wear a bullet proof vest at all times. He even went out and copped a bulletproof car, not to mention he was tired of riding around in that Benz all the time anyway. Capo was still looking for the man they called Cash. He wasn't worried though. He knew he would be bumping into the man soon. Capo just drove around the city trying to get his thoughts together. It was so much going on and he just needed a little time to himself. As Capo rode, he pulled out his cell phone and dialed Shekia's number.

"Hey Capo what's up?" she answered sounding as if she was in a good mood.

"Chilling," Capo replied. "I think I'mma need you to make that trip for me again in a day or two."

"No problem," she said. "I'm already in Miami. I had to handle a little something so just set everything up and I got you."

"Say no more," Capo said ending the call. Capo stopped for a red light and filled his foam cup with Vodka, then mixed orange juice in with it. All he was missing was his haze. Capo decided to make a detour to go get some weed.

\*\*\*

Cash and Dough Boy sat on the hood of Cash's car in the middle of the hood as the two sipped on some hard liquor and passed a blunt back and forth. "What is it looking like?" Cash asked handing the blunt to Dough Boy.
"Not to good" Dough Boy replied taking a deep pull from the blunt. "Little Dough getting weaker and weaker every day. I got a meeting with the doctor tomorrow."

"What them numbers looking like?" Cash asked.

"I don't know yet, but I know that bitch gon be high," Dough Boy said shaking his head. He knew the doctor was going to break his pockets, but for his son's life, he would pay whatever the cost was.

"How much you got from that clown Crazy Moe last night?" Cash said laughing at how easy of a lick that turned out to be.

"$9,000.00" Dough Boy said as he watched one of his young workers sell the drugs that they stole from other drug dealers. He didn't care how he had to get the money up for his son. Whatever he had to do, it would get done.

"Stop stressing," Cash said passing Dough Boy the blunt. "Already know we ain't gon let nothing happen to your lil man," he said as he saw an all-white B.M.W pull up with the music blasting. "Fuck is this?" Cash asked out loud as the headlights from the car made it hard for them to see.

Capo hopped out the B.M.W and walked straight over to the young hustler. "I need three ounces of Piff," he said giving the young hustler dap slipping the money in his hand. "And don't have me waiting all motherfucking day!" he yelled as he pulled out his iPhone and read a text message he had just received. Capo placed his cell phone back in its case and he looked up, but he couldn't believe his eyes. He quickly pulled his out his .9mm and fired four shots in Cash and Dough Boy's direction.

"Oh shit that's Capo," Cash said pulling his .40 cal from the small of his back as he and Dough Boy swiftly took cover behind Cash's car as they heard the bullets from Capo's gun pinging and sparking off the car. Shattered glass rained down on the top of their heads. Cash quickly aimed his gun straight up in the air and let off three shots to keep Capo at bay. When Capo heard the return gunfire he quickly back peddled, back to his whip and pulled off. Once Cash and Dough Boy heard Capo hop back in his car, they quickly sprung up from behind the parked car and opened fire on Capo's car as they watched it peel off. "Bitch ass nigga," Cash cursed as he and Dough Boy hopped in his ride and fled the scene.

"Faggot Motherfuckers," Capo huffed as he tossed his gun out the window as he hopped on the expressway. He was mad that he hadn't hit one of the gunmen, but the truth was he was caught off guard and not expecting to run into the men. However, he promised it would be shots fired on site each and every time the two bumped into one another. Just as Capo was about to breathe easy, he saw flashing lights in his rearview mirror. "Fuck!" he cursed as he pulled over to the shoulder of the road and placed his whip in park.

"Hands on the steering wheel!" The white undercover officer yelled shining the bright light from his flashlight in Capo's face.

"Don't move!" a black detective yelled as he crept up on the passenger side.

"I'm not moving," Capo said, looking at the detectives as if they were crazy. Next thing he knew the white detective snatched Capo out the front seat of the car and slammed him on the damp concrete. "What the fuck yo? I ain't even doing shit!" Capo yelled as he was being handcuffed. As he laid face down on the ground he watched, the two detectives search his car looking for anything they could find. Capo wasn't worried. He knew his ride was clean because he had just bought it two days ago.

"Look what I found," the white detective sang with an evil smirk on his face as he held a Ziploc bag full of cocaine in his hand. "Care to explain why you were riding around with this?"

"Fuck outta here," Capo huffed. "That shit ain't mine!"

"I found it in your car," the white detective said trying to make Capo seem like he was crazy. The NYPD was sick and tired of Capo and his crew and they planned on taking him down by any means necessary. "Whose drugs are these?" the white detective asked his partner."

"His," the black detective replied pointing at Capo. "We found it in his car," he said sticking with the lie.

"Fuck y'all crackers!" Capo yelled as he was roughly tossed in the back seat of the unmarked car.

"Say another word and it's going to be me and you!" The black detective threatened trying to show off for the white detective. Capo was about to give the black detective a piece of his mind, but when he saw three more cop cars pull up he decided to hold his tongue. Capo watched as all the cops gathered around in a huddle and began to talk amongst themselves for about ten minutes. He figured they were getting their story together so they could all be on the same page. Fifteen minutes later, the black detective and the white detective hopped in the unmarked car and they both had smirks on their faces as they started up the car and pulled off.

\*\*\*

Crazy Moe pulled up to the location where he and his crew always meet. On the outside, it looked like an abandoned building, but on the inside, Crazy Moe had an office area built inside along with an area for all his soldiers to hang out. He hopped out his Range Rover and went inside. As soon as he stepped foot inside, Crazy Moe saw all his goons standing around waiting for him.

"What's the word on the streets?" Crazy Moe asked as soon as he stepped foot in the joint. Two weeks had gone by, so by now he knew the hood had some kind of info for him. His main goon named Tiger walked up and gave it to him straight up. "The word is some cat from Capo's crew named Bone was the one who was behind the trigger," Tiger told him.

# THE TEFLON QUEEN

"Bone," Crazy Moe repeated. "Where can I find this clown?"

"It's this lounge Capo and his crew is at like every other night downtown. You want me and a few goons to run down there and air that shit out?" Tiger asked excitedly.

Crazy Moe thought about it for a second. At first he was about to say no, but he knew if he didn't retaliate then his crew would surely start to second-guess him. "Fuck it," Crazy Moe said. "Air that whole shit out!" he ordered as he watched Tiger and a few goons strap up and then head out the door to go handle their business.

"Fuck," Crazy Moe huffed. He was tired of living the way he was and after pretending to be a drug dealer, he couldn't understand how the real drug dealers did it; constantly looking over their shoulder for stickup kids, jealous niggaz, gold-diggers, snitches, how they survived during a drought, and the whole nine. The whole way they lived was way too much for him and he couldn't wait until he closed the case so he could go back to living his regular life, he thought as he hopped back in his Range Rover and headed back home. He really needed to just chill and relax in this game. It just seemed like he never got a day off. All the negative thoughts that was running through his brain, all disappeared and a smile spread across his face when he pulled up to his house and saw Angela's red Lambo parked in his drive way. Ever since the two had sex that night, they had been seeing each other every night. James had even given Angela her own set of keys to his house. When James stepped inside his house, he almost didn't recognize it. All of his old furniture had been replaced with all brand new furniture. He looked around and saw expensive leather couches all throughout his living room. There was brand new plush carpet on the floor throughout the whole house and his old 32 inch T.V had been replaced by a new 60 inch flat screen 3D T.V.

"Hey baby," Angela said coming from the kitchen wearing nothing but an expensive silk robe. "Do you like it?"

"Yes I love it," James said as he hugged Angela tightly. "Where did you get the money to afford this?" he asked.

"Hush," Angela said placing her finger on his lips. "You don't have to worry about money with me. I have plenty of it and from now on my man will only have the better things in life," she told him. "And since you didn't want to move to a bigger house, I just thought I'd hook this one up."

"I love it baby," James said. "Please just tell me you ain't doing anything illegal for this money."

Angela laughed. "Baby my parents left me money when they passed away," she told him. "Now sit down and relax. The food is almost ready," Angela said quickly changing the subject. She knew that James would ask questions when he got home so she made sure she had all her answers ready. Angela hated to have to lie to James but the truth was either she was going to lie to him or not deal with him at all. What started as just them hanging out had turned into the two falling in love. Angela hadn't planned for this to happen, but now that her feelings were involved, it was too late.

"What you cooking baby?" James yelled as he helped himself to a seat on the new leather couch.

"It's a surprise," Angela smiled as she grabbed the remote, pressed a button, and Kanye West flowed through the speakers. James relaxed and listened to the music as Angela came back and handed him a drink then disappeared back into the kitchen. As James sat on the couch, sipping from his drink all he could think about was closing the case. The more and more he thought about what Wayne doing to the black community was, the more he wanted to slap the cuffs on him.

"Okay it's ready," Angela said interrupting James' thoughts. Just as James hopped up off the couch, he heard his cell phone ringing. He looked at the caller I.D. and saw that it was Wayne calling. "What's up boss man?" he answered.

"I need you to swing by my office for a second," Wayne said ending the call. Once James hung up his phone, he looked up and saw Angela looking dead at him. "You gotta leave don't you?" she asked with a sad look on her face.

"Yes," James replied as he kissed Angela's lips. "Put my food in the microwave and I promise I'll eat it later," he said as he rushed out the door.

\*\*\*

Bone and Kim sat in their private booth in the back of the lounge seeing who could out drink the other. "When you going to get you a girlfriend and stop messing around with all these hoes?" Kim asked.

"Girlfriend?" Bone repeated looking at Kim as if she was insane. "Nah, I don't have time to be all tied down and shit. Bitch nagging me and all that. Nah, I ain't wit it," he said downing a shot. The truth was every time he got a girl he liked he would meet another girl he liked the next week so he just gave up on relationships to save himself the headache.

"I'm sure there's probably a nice girl out here for you," Kim laughed.

"Since you asking all these questions; I have a question for you," Bone said pouring himself another shot. "When you and Capo going to settle down?"

"Boy please," Kim said waving off him. "Me and Capo just cool. Besides he got too many hoes for me," she said as she saw Moose walking up with a serious look on his face.

"What's wrong?" Bone asked noticing that something was wrong.

"I just got the word that Capo is locked up," Moose reported.

"Who told you that?" Kim asked with a nervous facial expression. Instantly her stomach felt like she was going downhill on a roller coaster.

"Some fiend just told me," Moose replied. "He said when he was getting released he saw two detectives bringing Capo in." Kim immediately shot to her feet. "I'm going down to the station," she said as she finished her last shot then headed for the exit. Just as Kim was exiting the lounge, Tiger and three goons were making their way inside.

Bone sat in the booth listening to Moose telling him the rest of the story. He was only half listening as his eyes were on this nice little chocolate thing who was giving him the "what's good" eye. Bone motioned for the woman to come here with his hand. Moose looked, saw the young lady, and shook his head. "Man fuck that bitch," he huffed. "I say we should lay low until we hear from Capo."

"Capo's going to be fine," Bone said still not paying Moose any mind.

"Stop worrying so much," he said draping his arm around Moose. "You want me to see if shorty got a friend for you?" A loud blast caused Bone's whole body to jump as he saw Moose's body crumble to the floor as his blood leaked all over Bone's shoes. Bone immediately dropped down to the floor taking cover as he heard multiple gunshots being fired at the same time. He pulled out his 9mm and aimed it at the gunman. There were so many people running for their lives, scrambling to get out the lounge that Bone couldn't get a clear shot.

"Fuck it!" he cursed as he pulled the trigger anyway not caring who he hit. When two of Capo's goons on other side of the lounge saw what was going on, they quickly got involved in the gunfight. Tiger quickly spun around, waved his Mac-10 in the direction of the two goons, and took out both men including four other people who just happened to be in the wrong place at the wrong time. "We're out!" Tiger yelled as he and his team continued to fire as they back peddled out of the lounge.

# THE TEFLON QUEEN

Once the gunfire ended, Bone quickly jumped up and ran towards the exit. When he got outside, he saw four men running through the parking lot. He quickly aimed his gun at one of the men and let off four shots in his direction taking him down as the other three got away. When the gunfight was finally over, Bone rushed back in the lounge to where Moose's body lay. "Fuck!" Bone cursed looking down at Moose who was laid out with a hole in his forehead. Right then and there Bone knew that he would murder whoever was responsible for this.

*** 

Kim stepped in the police station and headed straight for the front desk. Behind the desk sat an angry looking black man. "How you doing sir," Kim said politely, but didn't get a response. "I said how you doing sir!" she repeated.

"Go sit down over there and give me one second!" The black man barked catching Kim off guard.

"Fuck you talking too like that?" Kim spat not liking how the officer behind the desk had addressed her. "Better act like you got some sense before you get touched up in here!"

The black officer slowly rose from his seat. "You threatening me?" said he asked loud enough so the whole lobby could hear him.

"Fuck you!" Kim huffed as she turned around and headed for the exit. "Uncle Tom Motherfucker!" Just as she was about to exit the police station, Kim saw Mr. Goldberg entering the building. "Hey Mr. Goldberg," she said as the two shook hands. "Are you here for Capo?"

"Yes," Mr. Goldberg answered. "Where is he?"

"I don't know," Kim huffed. "This clown behind the desk won't give me no info," she said as she watched Mr. Goldberg walk straight up to the officer behind the desk and seconds later, he was allowed in the back.

He looked back at Kim and held up a single finger signaling for her to give him one second.

\*\*\*

Capo sat in the holding cell with a few other inmates who had been arrested. Jail was nothing new to Capo. He had been down this road a few times so he knew the procedure well. "Fuck!" Capo cursed when he thought about how the crooked cops had planted the drugs in his car. He knew they couldn't take him down fair and square. *"How the fuck am I going to get out of this one?"* He thought as he sat down on the hard wooden bench. Ever since he and Wayne had fallen out, Capo noticed that his life was now so much harder. "I need a vacation," he said out loud, as he saw one of the guards enter the cell and hand out bologna sandwiches and a small carton of milk to each inmate. *"Nobody don't want this shit,"* Capo thought as he tossed his sandwich and milk on the bench. All he could think about was getting out of this place and going home so he could take a nice shower.

"A, yo my man," Capo heard a voice yell. He turned around and saw some filthy looking man trying to get his attention. "What?" Capo yelled back.

"Let me get that milk fam!" The man said aggressively looking in Capo's eyes looking for any signs of fear or weakness.

"Yo, did you just ask me could you have my milk?" Capo asked with his face crumbled up.

"Yeah," the man replied looking Capo in his eyes.

"Yeah you can have it. I don't even want this shit," Capo told him as he shook his head and sighed loudly. As soon as the man went to reach down for the milk, Capo stole on him catching him with a sharp uppercut that laid him out cold. "Nigga don't you…" Capo growled as he raised his foot and began stomping the man out. "Ever ask me for no

# THE TEFLON QUEEN

motherfucking milk!" He gave the man one last kick as he went and sat down on the bench. Minutes later, the white detective came back to the cell and got Capo.

"I have a few questions that I need to ask you. Come with me," he said as he led the way towards the interrogation room.

Capo sat in the back as the two detectives tried to break him down. He knew the rules and yawned loudly as he listened to the detective who was huffing and puffing. "I'm going to ask you one last time. Why were you out there shooting and who were you shooting at?"

"Shooting what?" Capo asked faking ignorance. The detective roughly grabbed Capo by his shirt, "Bitch you better stop playing with me and give me some answers. You can start by telling me where you got those drugs!"

"Get your fucking hands off me!" Capo huffed smacking the detective's hands from off his shirt. Before the detective could react, Mr. Goldberg busted through the door.

"What is going on in here?" he asked looking around.

"Nothing. We were just talking," the white detective whose name was Billy answered with a smirk.

"Come on lets go," Mr. Goldberg said to Capo, but his eyes stayed on Detective Billy as he and Capo made their exit. When Capo and Mr. Goldberg made it outside, Capo saw Kim leaning on the hood of her car waiting for him. He turned and looked at Mr. Goldberg. "Good looking," he said as the two shook hands. "I'll get the money that you put up for my bail back to you by tomorrow."

"You going to have to slow down," Mr. Goldberg began. "These crackers are not playing! They don't like you and can't wait to take you down."

Capo sucked his teeth. "Fuck them crackers!" he said fanning his hand. "Thanks again," he said over his shoulder as he walked off headed over to the car. Capo knew the cops were on a mission to erase him from off the streets, but at the same time, he knew Wayne was gunning for him along with Cash, Dough Boy, and Crazy Moe. Capo wanted to chill but at the same time, he planned on defending himself by any means necessary.

"What happened?" Kim asked as she ran up and hugged Capo tightly.

"Ran into those two clowns that ran down on us at the pool," Capo told her. "Had to air it out," he said as the two hopped in the car.

"We going to have to chill for a minute," Kim said as she pulled off. "Shit been kind of crazy out here on these streets. I say we should just go out of town and let the little homies hold down the streets for a few months," she suggested. Kim loved Capo but she knew if he didn't get out soon then it would soon be no way out for him.

"We gon think of something," Capo said as he stared out the window looking at the city pass him by.

\*\*\*

Crazy Moe parked his Range Rover in the driveway of Wayne's mansion and shut the car down. He grabbed his .45 that rested on the passenger seat and stuck it down in his waistband as he got out the vehicle and headed towards the front door.

"He's back in his office," Tank said in a deep voice. As Crazy Moe walked down the hallway to Wayne's office, he wondered what was so important because when Wayne had called him he could hear the stress in his voice. "What's up boss man?" Crazy Moe said stepping inside Wayne's office.

# THE TEFLON QUEEN

"Have a seat," Wayne said motioning for Crazy Moe to sit down with his hand. He poured himself a drink before he spoke. "I got this big ass shipment coming in next week," he paused so he could take a sip from his drink. "And from now on you are going to be the man in charge of getting the shit," Wayne said looking up at Crazy Moe. "Can you handle that?"

"Of course I can," Crazy Moe said confidently. "Just let me know what I need to do."

"Well usually Capo was the one who handled this for me, but since he's no longer around I'm going to need you to fill in for him" Wayne told him.

"I got you," Crazy Moe replied. This was just the opportunity he was waiting for. This was all he needed to put Wayne away forever. Crazy Moe made sure he sat straight up so that the wire he was wearing caught every word that Wayne had said.

"The only problem is, I'm going to have to come with you next week to make the pickup," Wayne told him. "These Chinese motherfuckers who I been doing business with don't trust a motherfucker and since they don't know you yet I have to come along with you so that they know they can trust you."

"I understand," Crazy Moe said, nodding his head. "Trust me I won't let you down."

"I know you won't cause if you ever do I will kill you," Wayne said seriously, but with a smile on his face.

"You have nothing to worry about," Crazy Moe said as he stood up to leave. "You can count on me."

"I better," Wayne said as he watched Crazy Moe leave. When Crazy Moe stepped foot back outside a smile quickly appeared across his face.

He knew he had Wayne right where he wanted him and finally he was about to close this case once and for all.

***

Dough Boy pulled up into the hospitals parking lot like a mad man. He hopped out his car and ran full speed inside the hospital. "Hey," he said out of breath to the woman who sat behind the counter. "My son just got rushed to this hospital and his name is Keith Washington. Can you please tell me what room he's in?"

The lady behind the desk punched a few keys on the key board then looked up and said, "Room 303."

"Thank you," Dough Boy said as he ran towards the staircase and took the steps. When he reached room 303 he saw his wife Monica sitting by Lil Dough's bed. "How is he?" Dough Boy asked. When Monica looked up and saw her husband standing there, she quickly got up and hugged him tightly. Just from the way she was hugging him, told Dough Boy it was bad. "Everything is going to be alright baby," he promised as he rubbed his wife's back.

"Excuse me Mr. Washington?" The doctor said interrupting the two.

"Can I have a word with you outside for a second?"

"I'll be right back," Dough Boy said as he kissed Monica then stepped outside so he and the doctor could talk. "Okay doc, give it to me straight up."

"Well it's simple," the doctor began. "If your son doesn't get a new heart soon he's going to die."

"Just let me know what I have to do doc and it's gonna get done," Dough Boy told him.

"Well once you get the money for the procedure then we can put him on the waiting list, but by the time your son's name come up it might be a little too late," the doctor replied. "Ain't no telling how long it will be before his name pops up."

"I have the money right now for the procedure," Dough Boy said desperately. "Is there any way to get around that waiting list?"

"Why yes there is," the doctor told him. "But it's going to cost you $100,000.00."

"$100,000.00?" Dough Boy echoed. "Come on doc you can't bring down the price just a little bit?"

"I'm afraid not. If I get caught doing this I can lose everything I've worked so hard for," the doctor replied. "Besides what I'm doing is illegal, but since I know how bad you need your son's name moved up on the list, I'm trying to look out for you."

Dough Boy looked back inside the room and saw his wife still crying. Ever since their son had been battling with this problem him and his wife had been taking it very rough. "I'll get you the money."

"Here's my card," the doctor said handing it to Dough Boy. "Whenever you're ready just give me a call," he said as he turned and walked away.

# CHAPTER 11

Shekia laid on a beach chair with her all-red swimsuit and dark Chanel shades as she watched Scarface ride his Jet Ski like a madman in the water. Shekia had been out in Miami with Scarface for the past two weeks. The two had been hanging out and getting to know one another. Shekia couldn't believe how cool Scarface was or how the two of them had so much in common.

"You don't wanna get in the water?" Scarface asked walking up dripping wet.

"No. I was having fun watching you," Shekia said looking at Scarface's chiseled body.

"I'm so sad that you have to leave me tonight," Scarface said with a smile, but on the inside he wasn't smiling. He didn't want Shekia to leave. He wanted her to move out to Miami with him, but he knew right now was too soon to ask and he would be rushing it.

"I know right," Shekia said giving Scarface her puppy face. "I wish I could stay," she said as she bobbed her head to Nicki Minaj's song "Your Love" which flowed from the speakers that sat on Scarface's back porch. Shekia was about to say something, but Scarface quickly hushed her by placing a single finger on her lips. She sat back and watched as Scarface untied the bottom to her swimsuit and removed it effortlessly. He quickly parted her legs and gently kissed on the magic button that rested between her thighs.

"Damn," Shekia moaned as she ran her fingers through Scarface's dreads and threw her head back in pleasure. Scarface licked, kissed, and sucked all over Shekia's clit as he slipped two fingers inside of her, forcing her to cum for him. Shekia wrapped her legs around Scarface's neck as her body shook uncontrollably.

"Just a little something for you to think about on that long ass ride back home," Scarface said smiling.

"You must be crazy," Shekia huffed. "You better give me some of that dick!" she demanded as she snatched off Scarface's shorts and hopped up off the beach chair.

"What you doing?" Scarface asked as Shekia pushed him down on the beach chair.

"I got this," she said with a seductive look on her face as she straddled him and slowly slipped him inside of her.

"That's right baby ride this dick," Scarface coached as he smacked her ass then placed one of her nice sized titties in his mouth. Shekia bounced up and down on Scarface as if she was trying to break his dick. All that could be heard was her moaning and her ass cheeks clapping every time she came down. The two then began kissing heavily while Shekia continued to bounce up and down until Scarface announced that he was about to cum. Shekia quickly hopped up off his dick just in time as he came all over his stomach.

"Damn," Shekia said out of breath. "Shit I wasn't prepared for all that," she laughed.

"I want you to come move out here with me," Scarface said getting straight to the point. All the girls he usually came across were strictly trying to get with him because he was paid, but he needed a woman who didn't want nothing from him, but his heart.

"You have everything you could possibly want and you can have any woman you want," Shekia said confused. "Why would you want to be with me? I'm a nobody."

"You're not a nobody," Scarface corrected her. "You are a beautiful woman and I would be honored if you came and allowed me to treat you like a queen." Truth be told Scarface needed a book smart woman and a woman that if things ever got messed up she wouldn't be too good to go out and help him get that money.

"So what you want me to just up and leave New York and move out here with you?" Shekia asked again just to make sure.

"Yes," Scarface said seriously.

"I would love to, but I would have to talk to Capo first," Shekia told him.

"Is that your man or something? If so my bad," Scarface said throwing his hands up in surrender.

"No, he's not my man, but I had agreed to make these runs for him and I don't just want to leave him hanging like that you know."

"I understand," Scarface said as the two walked back into the house butt naked. "Can you please just think about it and if you do decide to come out here then I'll handle Capo for you."

"Okay that sounds fair," Shekia said as the two went inside the master bedroom for round two before Shekia left.

\*\*\*

"Fuck going on over here?" Capo said as Kim pulled up in front of the lounge and saw cops all over the place. "Get Bone on the phone," he said as he watched Kim pull out her cell phone and dial Bone's number.

"Nigga where you at?" Kim said into the receiver. "A'ight stay right there. We on our way."

"Where's that fool at?" Capo said with an angry look on his face.

"At the strip club down the street," Kim replied as she pulled off heading to Bone's destination. When Kim pulled up in the strip club's parking lot, she spotted Bone sitting on the hood of one of the cars that sat in the parking lot. From the look on Bone's face Capo could tell that the news he was about to hear was sure to be bad.

"What happened over at the lounge?" Capo asked as soon as he stepped out the car.

"Niggaz ran down on me and Moose," Bone said nonchalantly.

"Where's Moose?" Kim asked.

"He ain't make it," Bone replied as he slipped a blunt in his mouth. "Motherfuckers came from all directions blasting!"

"You know who they were?" Capo asked.

"Word on streets is that it was a few of Crazy Moe peoples," Bone replied. He could care less who it was. The bottom line was whoever was responsible for Moose's death was going to die and he was going to make sure of it. "I'mma take care of it. Don't even worry about it," Bone assured him.

"Nah, nah, nah," Capo said taking the blunt from Bone's hand. "We have to chill. Too much heat has been coming down on us plus the NYPD is already on a mission to shut us down."

Bone crumbled up his face. "So we just going to let these niggaz slide?"

"Of course not," Capo told him. "We going to wait until this heat die down. Then we are going to take out each and every one of them niggaz." Capo could tell that Bone wasn't really feeling what he was saying, but he didn't care. "Can I trust you?"

# SILK WHITE

"Come on? How you gon ask me some shit like that?" Bone said taking a deep pull from the blunt. "If not me, then who?"

"Good, cause me and Kim going out of town for a little while so some of this heat can die down, but I'mma need you to hold shit down for me while I'm gone," Capo said looking closely at Bone to see how he was taking the news. "Shekia will be back in two days with the new package. Handle that and make it do what it do."

"When y'all supposed to be leaving?" Bone asked.

"At the end of the week," Capo replied. He knew if he wanted to stay out of jail, he didn't have long to disappear and get off of the cops radar.

"Let me throw y'all a little party before y'all leave," Bone suggested.

"Nah, I don't really want a lot of attention on me before I leave," Capo said knowing all eyes were going to be on him. "Stay focused on this business. That's all I need for you to do," he said as he gave Bone dap and him and Kim left the scene.

"Bitch ass nigga," Bone mumbled once Capo and Kim had pulled off. In his eyes, he felt that Capo was becoming weak and didn't deserve to call the shots anymore especially if he was going to let the people who murdered his friend slide as if nothing ever happened. "Motherfuckers always change when they make a little bit of money," he huffed as he hopped in his car and headed home. For the entire ride home Bone thought about going toe-to-toe with Capo for the throne. It was a hard decision for him to make because he still had love for the man, but in his heart, he felt that Capo was turning soft. *"In this business it's either kill or be killed,"* Bone told himself as he hopped out of his car and headed towards his front door. As soon as he stuck his key in the keyhole, Bone heard a clicking sound followed by the barrel of a gun being pressed to the back of his head.

"I dare you to move!" Dough Boy bark as he roughly grabbed Bone by the back of his neck and pressed the barrel of his .44 even deeper into the back of his head.

"Long time no see," Cash said as he walked up and removed Bone's gun from his waistband and then turned the key that was already in the lock and let himself in. Once inside the house, Dough Boy cracked Bone in the back of the head with his gun knocking him out instantly. Dough Boy then removed a pair of handcuffs and placed them on Bone's wrist.

"Let's find this money," Cash said. "I know he holding something up in here."

The two searched the house up and down until they found a bag full of money in Bone's closet. "Count that up," Cash said tossing the bag to Dough Boy as he walked back over to where Bone laid. "Where's ya boy Capo at?" he asked.

"Fuck you," Bone snarled. All he could think about was what he was going to do to these niggaz if he survived this.

"You just make sure you tell him that the next time he tries to run up on me, he better not miss," Cash said as he viciously kicked Bone in his face.

"$18,000.00" Dough Boy announced as he tossed Cash his half of the money.

"Nah," Cash said tossing the money back to Dough Boy. "You need that more than I do. Get little man what he needs."

"Good looking," Dough Boy said gladly accepting the funds. So far, he had $55,000.00 saved up, but his time was running out and he knew he would have to get the rest of that money up and do it fast.

"Catch you later," Cash laughed as him and Dough Boy left Bone handcuffed and laying on the floor in his own crib.

"How much you short?" Cash asked once the two had pulled away from Bone's crib.

"$45,000.00" Dough Boy replied.

"I got $20,000.00 at the crib. It's yours," Cash said as he hopped on the highway.

"Good looking! You know I'mma get that back to you when I get back on my feet," Dough Boy promised. He hated to have to borrow money from anybody, but right now, it didn't matter where he got the money. All he could think about was saving his son's life."

"Don't even worry about it," Cash smiled. "Capo and his crew is going to pay for everything. I got a little plan."

# CHAPTER 12

Crazy Moe sat on Wayne's couch as he waited for him to come down stairs. He had been waiting for since he started working on this case this day. He was finally about to take Wayne off the streets for good. He just hoped that it would be an easy take down. He didn't want to shoot anybody but he definitely would if he had too. As Crazy Moe sat on the couch, he saw Tank make his way down the stairs first. "Wayne will be down in a minute."

"A'ight bet," Crazy Moe replied. He already had a gang of agents surrounding the pickup spot hours before the pickup and drop was even scheduled to go down. About ten minutes later, Wayne came downstairs with a smile on his face. "You ready to get this money?"

"I'm always ready for that," Crazy Moe said returning Wayne's smile.

"I'm about to introduce you to the big leagues. Don't let me down you hear," Wayne said looking Crazy Moe in his eyes.

"We don't drop no balls over here," Crazy Moe said cockily. That last comment put a smile on Wayne's face.

"Let's get up outta here and handle this business," Wayne said as the trio hopped in the Navigator that awaited them. The ride to the destination was a quiet one until Crazy Moe's phone rung. He looked at the caller I.D. and saw Angie's name flashing across the screen. "Hey baby what's up?" he answered.

"Hey baby did I catch you at a bad time?" Angela asked sounding as if she was in a good mood.

# SILK WHITE

"Yes baby I am a little busy right now," Crazy Moe told her. "Is something wrong?"

"No baby just wanted to hear your voice and tell you that I love you," Angela said.

"I love you too baby. I'll call you later," Crazy Moe said ending the call. When he hung up, he saw Tank peeking at him through the rearview mirror.

"Circle this bitch twice before we go in there," Wayne instructed once Tank reached the warehouse. As Tank circled the building twice, Crazy Moe felt the butterflies began to form in his stomach.

"We straight boss," Tank said as he pulled into the warehouse. When they pulled inside, they saw about ten to twelve Chinese men standing in front of four all-black trucks.

"Let's do this," Wayne said as him and Tank hopped out of the truck. Crazy Moe flipped switch on his cell phone that allowed the other agents to be able to hear everything that was going on as he also hopped out the truck.

"What's up Lee?" Wayne said with a smile as the two men shook hands. "Long time no see."

"Long time no see is right," the Chinese man said focusing his attention on the new guy. "Where did you find this guy at?" Lee asked suspiciously, as he looked Crazy Moe up and down.

"He's cool," Wayne said vouching for Crazy Moe. "I wouldn't bring anybody here that will harm you or me for that matter," Wayne assured him. "Now let's get down to business."

"Not so fast," Lee said as he gave one of his security guards a head nod. Immediately, the guard walked up to Crazy Moe. "Lift up your shirt," he said looking Crazy Moe straight in his eyes.

"Come on Lee what kind of shit is this?" Wayne complained. "You are disrespecting me right now."

"Business is business," Lee countered quickly.

"Nah its cool," Crazy Moe said as he lifted up his shirt and spun around so Lee and his men could see that he wasn't wearing a wire.

"Now can we get on with this?" Wayne said with an angry look on his face. He couldn't believe how Lee had disrespected him asking to see if Crazy Moe was wearing a wire. Since he was with Wayne that was just as bad as Lee asking Wayne was he wearing a wire.

"No disrespect," Lee apologized. "But I have to be sure who I'm dealing with."

Wayne sighed loudly. "Whatever let's just get this business over with so I can go," he said as he walked over to his SUV and retrieved the duffle bag full of money. "Let me guess, you wanna count this too right?" Wayne said sarcastically as he tossed the duffle bag at Lee's chest. Lee caught the duffle bag and smiled.

"Once you start making tons of money with this new product, I'm sure you will find a way to forgive me," he joked as he signaled for one of his security guards to give Wayne the drugs. Tank took the two duffle bags from the Chinese man's hands and placed them in the Navigator.

"It's always a pleasure," Lee said with a smile as he extended his hand.

# SILK WHITE

"Fuck you Lee," Wayne replied as the two men shook hands. Just as each man was about to hop back in their vehicles, a loud explosion erupted, followed by several cars entering the warehouse.

"F.B.I, nobody move!" one of the agents yelled.

"What the fuck?" Wayne asked confused as he pulled his 9mm from his waistband and sent a shot in the agent's direction. Once that shot went off, everybody who had a gun began shooting. Crazy Moe quickly took cover behind the SUV and pulled out his .45. He spotted Lee trying to run toward the exit all the way in the back of the warehouse.

Crazy Moe got on one knee and aimed his weapon at the moving target. He pulled the trigger and watched as Lee grabbed the back of his thigh and hit the floor. Wayne hopped in the Navigator and gunned the engine. The F.B.I agents fired almost 100 rounds into the Navigator until it finally came to a stop. Crazy Moe saw Tank creeping up on one of the agents from behind. He quickly raised his gun and put a bullet in the back of Tank's head killing him instantly. The agents quickly arrested Lee and all his men. When they removed Wayne from his truck, they found that he had only been hit once in the shoulder and twice in the leg.

"You fucking crackers!" Wayne said wincing in pain as they dragged him out of the vehicle, handcuffed him, and then placed him on a stretcher.

"I'll be out in a week," Wayne said as he spit blood in the head F.B.I Agent's face then busted out laughing. The agent wiped his face and smiled. "I'd like to introduce you to someone Mr. Wayne," the head agent said returning Wayne's smile. "I'd like to introduce you to Agent James Carter," he said as he draped his arm around James' neck.

"Get the fuck outta here," Wayne said flashing a bloody smile. "Fuck is he talking about?" he asked looking at James. When James eyes went directly to the floor, Wayne automatically knew he was fucked. "You're a motherfucking cop? Huh? Answer me you bitch!" he yelled as an agent rolled him towards the awaiting ambulance. "You're a dead man!" Wayne yelled. "You hear me, a dead man!"

"You did great," the head agent said as he shook James' hand. "You probably are going to get a medal for this one."

James smiled and deep down he was happy he had got a man like Wayne off the streets. He felt like a traitor, but this was his job and he was the best at what he did for a reason.

"Let's go out and celebrate," the head agent announced. "Drinks on me!"

***

Angela sat in the house lying across the couch flicking through the channels. *"What the hell is going on?"* she thought out loud when she saw breaking news on every channel.

"This is Lisa reporting live from channel 2 news," the reporter announced. "I'm standing outside of the warehouse where drug kingpin Wayne Murray was just taken down by authorities. Word is when authorities tried to take Murray down, him and his crew opened fire. We don't have the full story yet, but what we do know is that Wayne Murray has been shot and rushed to the hospital. This is Lisa Turner reporting live from Channel 2 News."

"Oh shit," Angela said as she sat up on the couch. She continued to listen to the news so she could get more info. Seconds later, James walked inside the house carrying an expensive bottle of champagne.

"Damn this shit is on every channel," he said when he walked in and looked at the T.V.

"You heard about what happened?" Angela asked.

# SILK WHITE

"Heard about it? I was there," James said with a smile. "I finally closed the case baby," he said holding up the bottle of champagne.

"Congratulations," Angela said forcing a smile to appear on her face. She loved James with all of her heart, but she hated what he did for a living. Her love for him made her overlook what he did for a living.

"They are going to give me a medal for this and a promotion," James announced.

"I'm so happy for you baby," Angela said as she slid in his arms and hugged him tightly. James lifted her up and she quickly wrapped her legs around his waist. "Let's go upstairs and celebrate," James whispered in her ear as he carried her off to the bedroom.

***

Capo and Kim sat in the crib counting their money as they both bobbed their heads to Young Jeezy's new album. "This nigga killing this shit," Kim said as she passed the blunt over to Capo.

"Word," Capo agreed. He was excited about the trip that he and Kim were about to take. They didn't even know where they were going to go. They were going to decide when they made it to the airport. A knock at the door caused Capo to jump. Ever since he had bailed out, he had been super paranoid. "Go see who that is," he ordered. Kim grabbed the 9mm that was in arms reach on the table as she got up and made her way over to the door. Kim looked through the peephole and quickly slid her gun in the small of her back as she unlocked the door. Bone stepped in the crib with an angry look on his face.

"Fuck you doing on this side of town?" Capo asked with a smirk on his face.

# THE TEFLON QUEEN

"It's on!" Bone huffed as he sat down at the table along with Capo and Kim. "These nigga ran up on me the other night and took all my shit!"

"Who?" Capo asked.

"Cash and that nigga Dough Boy," Bone replied. "And he even had your chain on," he added.

"Word?" Capo said trying to hide how pissed he was. He had been hearing that Cash was out stunting with his chain on acting as if he was that nigga. "How you let them niggaz run down on you like that?"

"Niggaz snuck up on me from behind while I was going in my house," Bone said. "But I ain't worried because I got the word on where that nigga Cash rest his head. So just let me know what you wanna do?"

"I'm not really worried about that right now," Capo replied. Of course he wanted to kill Cash, but now wasn't the time. He was already out on bail and under a microscope and a murder charge was something he could do without right now. "I'm just focused on us leaving town right now."

"This nigga walking around with your chain on and you ain't worried about that right now?" Bone asked skeptically.

"You wouldn't understand," Capo said knowing Bone wouldn't understand even if he tried to explain it to him.

"*Bitch ass nigga,*" Bone thought as he accepted the blunt from Kim. "But anyway," he said changing the subject. "I set up a little going away get together for y'all tonight."

"Yo, didn't I tell you I didn't want no party?" Capo said as if Bone was becoming an annoyance.

"Nah, it's not a party," Bone lied. "It's going to be like a little get together."

"I don't know," Capo said, knowing if the word got out that it would be hundreds of people at the so called get together.

"Only about twenty people, if that will be there," Bone said lying with a straight face. He knew if he didn't lie it was no way Capo would show up especially now since he been acting like a bitch.

"We'll be there," Kim said as she stood up. "But you have to go cause we have a few things that we need to do," she said escorting him to the door.

"A'ight I'll see y'all later," Bone said as he made his exit.

"You think that nigga been acting funny lately?" Kim asked when she made it back to the table.

"What you mean?" Capo asked.

"I mean," Kim began. "He been acting a little funny don't you think?"

"Nah, I haven't noticed anything," Capo told her.

"Just keep a close eye on him," Kim said not liking the way Bone had been acting lately.

"I got you," Capo said as he stood up.

"Where you going?"

"Gotta go meet Shekia," Capo said looking at his watch. "She should be here in about an hour."

# THE TEFLON QUEEN
***

Shekia got back to New York and headed straight for the location that Capo had instructed her to meet him at, but during the whole ride home, all she could think about was what Scarface had asked her. Shekia was really feeling Scarface but she wasn't sure if it was love on his end or lust. She couldn't understand why Scarface would want her out of all the girls in the world. Then on top of everything, he wanted her to just up and move all the way to Miami and at this moment, Shekia wasn't sure if she was ready for such a big move. She pulled up into the KFC parking lot and placed the car in park as she sat and waited for Capo to arrive. Ten minutes later, Capo pulled up in a hooptie.

"What's up yo?" Capo asked with a smile as he got out the car and leaned on the hood.

"Everything is good," Shekia said giving Capo a pound. At first, she thought Capo was going to be a mean pain in the ass, but after getting to know him, she found out that he was really just a cool guy.

"So what's going on with you and Scarface?" he asked.

"Nothing; we just have been hanging out getting to know one another," Shekia said smiling just at the sound of Scarface's name.

"Scarface is a cool dude," Capo told her. "Make sure you take care of my man."

Shekia laughed. "He wants me to move out there with him, but I told him I would think about it because I didn't know how long you needed me to continue to making these runs for you. Besides the money you pay me is good," she said honestly.

"I mean," Capo began. "If you want to make that move you have all my support. All I ask is that you give me a month's notice."

# SILK WHITE

"Not a problem," Shekia said with a smile.

"I'm going to be leaving town in two days for a little while, so I'm going to leave Bone in charge of everything," Capo told her.

"How long you going to be gone?" Shekia asked.

"Until this heat die down, but I have a court date in two months so you never know," Capo replied. "But we supposed to be having a little get together tonight. You should stop by."

"Nah, I don't think so. I haven't seen my mother in a while so I think I'mma just shoot over there," Shekia told him. "I know she's probably worried sick about me."

"A'ight well if you change your mind you are more than welcome to swing through," Capo said as he grabbed both of Shekia's hands and pulled her in for a hug, but when the two touched hands, they smoothly exchanged car keys. "Call me later," Capo said as he hopped in the rental car and Shekia hopped in the hooptie.

When Shekia stepped foot inside her mother's house, she saw Ms. Pat sitting on the couch in the living room. The look on her mother's face told Shekia that she had an attitude.

"Where the fuck you been Shekia?" Ms. Pat asked, not even bothering to look at her daughter.

"Out minding my business," Shekia countered as she walked into the kitchen and poured herself some juice.

"I know you saw me calling you?" Ms. Pat said as she followed Shekia in the kitchen. "You still out there helping those boys sell their drugs aren't you?"

# THE TEFLON QUEEN

"For your information I was out with my new man, if you must know," Shekia said snaking her neck playfully.

"He must be no good too," Ms. Pat huffed. She had met all of Shekia's other boyfriends in the past, but now out the blue she had a new man, that she hadn't brought around to meet her mother. Instantly, Ms. Pat knew something wasn't right about her daughter's new man.

"So tell me about this new boyfriend of yours."

"You mad nosey," Shekia said defensively. "I'm not a child anymore. I don't have to bring every man I decide to talk to home to meet you. Like come on. I'm not in high school no more!"

"I see," Ms. Pat said as she went to her room and slammed the door behind her. Shekia sat on the couch and just shook her head. If her mother kept on acting like this, she was going to be moving to Miami sooner than expected.

# CHAPTER 13

Kim pulled up to the club and couldn't believe her eyes. The line to get into the "Get Together" was around the corner and there were people all around the club. There were even people in the parking lot getting their parking lot pimp on.

"I thought this motherfucker said it was only going to be twenty to thirty people here?" Capo asked from the passenger seat. Kim just shook her head.

"What you wanna do?"

"Fuck it," Capo shrugged his shoulders. "We already here so we might as well get our party on before we leave."

"Fuck it lets do it," Kim agreed as the two hopped out of her Lexus and made their way towards the entrance of the club. Capo walked up to the front door dressed in all black with three chains hanging from his neck. His all black attire made his jewelry stand out even more. Just as Capo and Kim were about to enter the club, a big swollen neck bouncer stepped in their path.

"Fuck y'all think y'all going?" the bounce asked folding his muscular arms across his chest.

"We just trying to get our party on fam," Capo said respectfully.

"That's what the line is for asshole!" the bouncer barked purposely trying to make a scene. Capo was about to reach for the .45 that rested on his waist, but decided against it. He knew nothing good was going to come from that.

"This party is for me and my friend here," Kim said trying another approach.

"Listen the only person who can tell me y'all don't have to get in line is Bone," the bouncer said cockily. Capo was about to inform the bouncer that Bone worked for him, but he didn't want to belittle Bone in the process.

"Fuck this shit," Capo said reaching for his hip as Kim quickly stopped him as she notice Bone step out the front door.

"Bone!" Kim called his name. "Yo tell this ugly motherfucker to move out of our way."

"Yo Pete they cool let them through," Bone told the bouncer. Capo stared the bouncer down as him and Kim followed Bone inside.

"Yo I thought you said this was going to be a small get together?" Capo barked not liking how the night had begun.

"The word spread like wildfire," Bone said shrugging his shoulders. "Fuck it, it is what it is!" As soon as the trio stepped foot inside the club, the sound of Wacka Flocka bumping through the speakers had everyone in the club hype and bouncing around. Not even ten seconds had passed and already Capo's shoes had been stepped on more times than he could count. Kim saw the aggravated look on Capo's face and immediately grabbed his hand and guided him through the crowded club over towards the V.I.P section, but it was even crowded over there as well.

"Let's just make the best of this," Kim smiled. "Just know after this we are outta here."

"You right baby," Capo said returning her smile. Capo loved to party, but now was a different story. He could tell by how crowded the club was that something was going to pop off and right now Capo

SILK WHITE

couldn't afford any unnecessary problems. He flicked his wrist and glanced at his watch. "An hour and I'm out," he told himself.

"Shout out to my man Capo I see you baby," the DJ announced over the mic as a spotlight landed on Capo and Kim for a few seconds. Capo quickly leaned over and whispered in Kim's ear. "We not going to be here long." Kim nodded her head signaling that she agreed with him.

Seconds later, Bone entered the V.I.P section with one of the bartenders behind him. "Thanks sweetheart," Bone smiled at the sexy bartender as he removed the bucket filled with bottles from her hand. Bone reached in the Rosay bucket, removed a bottle of Rosay, and handed it to Capo. "This is your night!"

"Yeah some night," Capo said accepting the bottle. He made sure he took slow sips to make sure that he wasn't too drunk and he could still be on point. As he sipped, he watched Bone for a second. Ever since Kim had told him to keep an eye on Bone, he had been noticing that Bone was starting to spread his wings a little more and he poked his chest out more than he used to. "Yo I'm ready to go," Capo said yelling in Kim's ear over the loud music.

"Okay let me go to the bathroom real quick," Kim replied as she downed the rest of her drink then snaked her way through the crowd heading towards the bathroom.

"What's wrong?" Bone yelled draping his arm around Capo's neck. "Loosen up champ."

"Nah, I'm about to get up outta here," Capo told him.

"Why? What's wrong?" Bone asked looking at Capo as if he was crazy.

"You just got here. Plus, look at all these hoes up in here."

"I'm just going to lay low until all this heat blows over and until this case is over," Capo informed him.

"Nigga you beat every case them crackers tried to pin on you," Bone said looking at Capo as if he had just drunk some spoiled milk. "You changing…"

"Changing?" Capo echoed, as he turned and got all up in Bone's face. "Changing how?"

"The old Capo I know would take these crackers head on; not run away from them like a coward," Bone huffed. Capo smirked as he took another swig from his bottle. "When you get knee deep like I am, then you'll understand where I'm coming from young blood, but until then just sit back and enjoy life."

"Whatever!" Bone said as he walked off and disappeared in the crowd. Capo thought about showing Bone ain't nothing changed by fucking him up right then and there, but for some reason he decided against it.

Kim exited the bathroom and squeezed her way back through the crowd over towards the V.I.P section. As she made her way through the crowd, she felt some one grab her wrist. "Damn! Ma, where you rushing too?" The voice asked. "Can I get a dance?"

"No, not right now," Kim said as she looked up and stopped dead in her tracks when she saw Capo's diamond "C" chain hanging around the man's neck.

"Where you rushing to?" Cash asked still holding on to Kim's wrist. He didn't recognize her, because of her clothes and makeup.

"I got my man over there waiting for me," Kim said smiling openly as she slid her hand in her pocket and removed a small razor.

"Fuck that nigga," Cash said hating. "You want me to go over there and snuff that nigga for you? Matter of fact," Cash said looking around.

"Where's that nigga at right now?" Before he got a chance to say another word Kim quickly raised her hand and brought it down hard slicing the side of Cash's face.

"Bitch!" Cash yelled as he turned and punched Kim in the face sending her stumbling backwards into other partygoers until she hit the floor. Kim crawled backwards on the floor as she saw Cash remove something from his waistband and move in for the kill. A man who had witnessed what had happened quickly stepped in.

"Why don't you try hitting a man like that?"

Cash felt his own blood dripping down his face and raised his arm dropping the man with two shots to the chest. Once the shots went off, everybody in the club went scrambling to get out the club alive. Kim quickly did her best to blend in with the crowd as she ran towards the nearest exit. Cash pushed other party goers out of his way trying to get a good shot at Kim as he moved as fast as he could a few feet behind her.

Capo stood in the V.I.P section bobbing his head to the sound of Yo Gotti bumping through the speakers. He took a swig from his bottle when he heard two thunderous shots blast throughout the club. He looked in the direction that the shots came from and saw Kim being chased by Cash whose face was covered in blood. Immediately, Capo pulled his .45 from his waistband and hopped over the rail. He landed on the dance floor, but couldn't get a good shot at Cash because of all the people stampeding over one another. Capo thought about just airing the whole shit out, but thought about the consequences. "Fuck this shit!" he huffed as he pulled the trigger not caring who he hit. "POW! POW! POW! POW! Instantly, the whole club got low once again. Cash looked up and saw Capo moving through the crowd with a gun in his hand. Cash began to back-peddle as he fired into the crowd. Neither man cared who they hit. When Cash made it outside, he quickly dashed for his car. He looked over to his left and saw Kim jogging towards him holding something shiny in her hand. Seconds later, he heard shots being fired back to back. Cash quickly took cover behind a parked car as he caught his breath. "Fuck!" he cursed as he touched his face and his hand came away bloody.

Capo came out of the club and saw Kim hunched down low easing her way over towards a parked car. He quickly ran over and joined her.

"Fuck it!" Cash yelled as he got up and made a run for it. Just as he was about to make it out of the parking lot, he felt a bullet pierce through the back of his thigh. "Awww shit!" he growled as he hit the pavement and gripped the back of his thigh. Capo and Kim walked in for the kill until they saw cop cars coming from every direction surrounding Cash.

"Come on we're out," Capo said as he grabbed Kim and forced her back to back the car.

"Get the fuck off of me!" Kim yelled as she struggled to get free from Capo's grip. Capo forcefully tossed Kim in the whip and slammed the door. He quickly ran around the car, hopped in the driver's seat, and put the pedal to the medal.

"You should have let me kill that motherfucker!" Kim huffed looking at the black bruise up under her eye.

"The cops were right there," Capo told her looking through the rearview mirror as he hopped on the highway. "I clapped that nigga for you. We'll catch him the next time."

"Fuck a next time!" Kim spat. "We had him right there!"

Capo didn't reply. He knew that Kim was upset, and decided to let her cool off first before he tried to talk to her. When the two walked in the house, they both stopped in front of the T.V. as they watched Crazy Moe received an award on the news.

"What the fuck?" Capo whispered as he saw the mayor of the city give Crazy Moe an award for taking down Wayne. "Get the fuck outta here!" he said in disbelief. "That nigga is a cop?"

"Can't trust nobody nowadays," Kim said shaking her head in disgust.

# CHAPTER 14

Angela laid across the king-sized bed wearing nothing but a thong, as she watched James receive an award, and get a promotion on the news. "Damn" she said to herself. The way they were praising James on T.V. Angela knew he had to be good at what he did. James Carter was just like Angela. The only difference was they played for different teams. Angela took a sip from her wine glass as she saw James enter the bedroom. "Hey baby" Angela sang as she jumped up and slid in James arms. "I was watching you on T.V."

"How'd I looked?" James asked as he and Angela engaged in a long sloppy kiss.

"My man always looks good," Angela boasted. "You know I don't play that shit."

"I'm happy to be home," James said as he took the wine glass from Angela's hand and flopped down on the bed. He knew after one big case that the next one wasn't far behind, he could only imagine what was waiting in the wings for him. "I'm just going to take this time to relax until the next big case comes up" he paused. "Knowing my luck I'll probably be assigned to a new case before the week is out."

Angela rubbed the back of James's head. "Baby you the best and that's what comes with the territory, but just know that I'll always have your back one hundred percent," she said slowly sliding down to her knees. Angela pulled down James pants and was glad to see that his dick was already at attention and ready for action. "Did you miss mami?" She asked talking to James' dick as she slowly kissed on the head before she took him fully into her mouth.

"Damn baby," James groaned with his eyes closed as he guided the back of Angela's head with his hand. He watched as Angela made his dick disappear then reappear. Once James felt himself about erupt he quickly stood up and bent Angela over, and slid her thong over to the side. Angela grabbed on to the edge of the dresser as she cocked her ass up in the air. "Yes daddy," she purred as she felt James enter her walls. Angela loved how James put it down in the bedroom. He knew exactly how she liked to be pleased and he always took care of his business. Once the two were all done, Angela laid her head on James' chest as the two fell fast asleep.

In the middle of the night, Angela was awoken by her cell phone ringing. "Hello?" She answered in a half sleep voice.

"Hey Angela it's me Mr. Goldberg" he said. "I'm sorry to wake you, but I need to see you in my office," Angela looked at the clock that rested on the nightstand that read 5:28 am.

"What you doing in the office right now?"

"Got a lot of work to do" Mr. Goldberg told her. "But I would appreciate it if you could be here as soon as possible."

"Getting dressed now," Angela said, ending the call. Angela slid out of bed and hopped in the shower. As she let the hot water massage her body, she wondered what Mr. Goldberg wanted with her, but she knew it had to be business because when Mr. Goldberg called nine times out of ten it was time to put that work in. She hopped out the shower, and threw on a cream, expensive business suit, pulled her hair back in a ponytail, then grabbed her purse.

"Where are you going baby?" James asked with his back turned in the bed.

"My lawyer just called me and asked me to come to his office," Angela replied. "He said had something important to talk to me about."

"Need me to come with you?" James asked with concern.

# THE TEFLON QUEEN

"No baby I'll be fine" Angela said as she gave James a kiss, then headed out the door.

***

"Where the fuck is this nigga?" Dough Boy thought out loud. Sitting in a stolen Acura, he had been waiting for his partner to show up for about two hours. Cash was never late for a job, so immediately Dough Boy hoped that his partner/best friend was all right. It had been three days since the two spoke. Every time Dough Boy tried to call Cash, his phone went straight to voicemail. "Where the fuck you at?" Dough Boy huffed. Just as he was getting ready to pull off, he heard his cell phone ringing. The only two people who had his number was Cash, and his wife, and he had just spoke to her ten minutes ago so it could only be one other person.

"Hello?" He yelled into the phone.

"Yo what's good?" Cash said into the phone.

"What's good my ass," Dough Boy barked. "Where the fuck you been. I been trying to call you all motherfucking week!"

"I'm locked up right now," Cash told him. "Bumped into Capo and his crew again, at some club and I had to let them thangs fly."

"Damn!" Dough Boy said shaking his head. "What they trying to hit you with?"

"Murder," Cash said sadly. "But I'mma beat that though, the bullets from my gun ain't the one that killed those people, but regardless I'm going to have to do some time."

"Damn I'm sitting out here in front of this chick's crib waiting for you."

"Fuck it!" Cash said. "One man don't stop the show, so continue on with the plan, and go get that money," he told him especially since he knew Dough Boy really needed the money.

"A'ight hold ya head in there," Dough Boy said. "And I'll have something for your books at the end of the week.

"Say no more" Cash said as he ended the call.

Dough Boy hung up the phone and cursed loudly. Ever since he started doing stickups, he always had Cash to watch his back. This was the first time he would have to put in work by himself.

"Time to go," Dough Boy said to himself as he slipped his fingers in his black gloves, cocked back his 9mm, and slid out the car headed towards the front door of the house he had been staked out in front of. Dough Boy aimed his 9mm at the lock, pulled the trigger, and then kicked in the front door. He rushed inside and saw an older woman washing dishes in the kitchen. When the woman saw the gunman enter her home, fear crept through her whole body as she dropped the dish that she held in her hand.

"Get over here bitch!" Dough Boy growled as he roughly grabbed the woman by the back of her neck and tossed her down to the floor, where he placed his knee in the middle of her back as he tied her hands behind her back with a roll of duct tape. "Don't fucking move!" Dough Boy yelled as he searched the rest of the house, just to make sure he and the older woman were the only two in the house. After searching the whole house, Dough Boy flopped down on the couch and turned the T.V. on making himself at home.

\*\*\*

Angela pulled up in front of Mr. Goldberg's office building as the sounds of Aaliyah bumped through her speakers. She sang along as she parked in the empty spot. Angela made her way inside the building and immediately the receptionist informed her that Mr. Goldberg was in his office waiting for her.

"Thank you," Angela said with a smile as she headed straight to the back. She stepped in Mr. Goldberg's office and saw him sitting behind his desk pouring himself a drink, as he sniffed a line of coke.

"Take it easy," Angela joked as she helped herself to a seat. "Now what's so important, that you calling me at the crack of dawn?"

"It's not looking too good," Mr. Goldberg began. "I know you heard they finally caught Wayne right?"

"Yeah I saw that on the news about a week or so ago," Angela replied. Inside she kind of felt guilty because her man was the one who was responsible for putting Wayne behind bars.

"I've been getting calls from Mr. Biggz all morning," Mr. Goldberg told her. "So it looks like you going to be pretty busy for the next few months."

Mr. Biggz was the man who paid for and set up all of Angela's contracts. He would always forward messages through Mr. Goldberg because he knew that was the only way the F.E.D.S could not eavesdrop on his calls, because it was illegal for them to listen to a conversation between one and his or her lawyer. "But the real reason I called you down here," Mr. Goldberg continued. "Was because Wayne called me and asked me to tell you to go and visit him today, he said he had something real important to talk to you about."

"Where are they holding him?" Angela asked.

"Rikers Island," Mr. Goldberg replied. "I think he's in O.B.C.C"

"Did he say what he wanted?"

"No," Mr. Goldberg told her. "He just said to tell you to come see him today."

"A'ight" Angela said as she stood up to leave. "If you hear from Mr. Biggz you know how to find me," she said as she exited his office. Angela got outside and quickly hopped in her car and headed straight to Rikers Island.

*** 

Wayne sat in his cell looking up at the ceiling in deep thought. He still couldn't believe that Crazy Moe turned out to be a federal agent. He had put all his trust in him and that person had turned around and fucked him over in the end. Wayne had time to think about the whole situation repeatedly, and no matter how many times he thought about it, he just couldn't seem to get the nasty taste of being played out of his mouth. Wayne knew it was no way for him to get out of this situation, but he knew if his life was over, he was definitely bringing a lot of people with him. Wayne laid on his bed with his hands folded behind his head, when he heard the C.O. bang on his cell door. "You got a visitor," the big C.O. announced. Wayne quickly hopped up off of his bed and followed the C.O. to the bubble where the C.O. handed him a pass, and allowed him to make his way to the visiting room. When Wayne finally reached the visiting area, he immediately had to strip down to his draws, and was handed a grey jumpsuit by another inmate that had the letters D.O.C. (Department Of Corrections) on the back. Wayne made his way out to the dance floor (visiting room) and immediately spotted Angela sitting over at the table in the corner looking sexy as usual.

"Thanks for coming" Wayne whispered in Angela's ear as he hugged her tightly taking a deep sniff of her perfume.

"Not a problem" Angela said as the two took their seats. From the look on Wayne's face, she could tell that he had been inside stressing. "You alright?"

# THE TEFLON QUEEN

"I'm good," Wayne replied with a smile. "Just trying to come to the understanding that I'm going to spend the rest of my life in a cell, trust me I'll be fine."

"You play and sometimes you gotta pay," Angela said repeating what her mentor told her a long time ago.

"Fuck all that," Wayne said ready to get down to business. "Why I called you down here is because a lot of people have to pay," he said. "Motherfuckers wanted to help take my life, now I'm about to return the favor" Wayne spat.

"Just let me know what you need me to do," Angela said already knowing that this was what this visit was all about.

"The first motherfucker I need you to get rid of for me is that crooked ass D.A. Heather, she's the first one I want to go. Number two on my list is that racist ass Judge Michael Steward. I want you to make his death a nasty one," Wayne told her with a serious look on his face. "And last but not least I need you to take care of that bitch ass faggot James Carter!" Wayne fumed. "That motherfucker has to go point blank! I'll pay whatever to make that happen; besides I already spoke to Mr. Biggz and he's already been paid, which means you've already been paid! All I wanted was for you to tell me in my face that you would handle these things for me."

"I got you," Angela said forcing a smile on her face, but deep down inside she wanted to cry. She knew this day would eventually come, and she didn't even want to think about hurting the man that she was so madly in love with.

"You sure you can handle all three?" Wayne asked just to be on the safe side. Angela gave him a you gotta be kidding me look. "As long as the money right it'll get done," she stated plainly.

# SILK WHITE

"The money's already there so you should be getting a call from either Mr. Biggz or Mr. Goldberg tonight or tomorrow."

"No problem." Angela said as she stood up to leave. Wayne quickly stood up and hugged her again. "Make sure when you take out James, that it makes the news so I can see it," he whispered in her ear.

"Consider it done," Angela said with a smirk as she turned and made her exit. When she retrieved her cell from out of the locker, she saw that she had three text messages from Mr. Goldberg confirming everything Wayne had just told her. One of the text informed her that the money for all three of the contracts was already in her account. Angela hopped back in her car and shook her head. Business was business and she had never unfulfilled a contract and didn't plan on starting now.

When Angela made it back home, she walked in her bedroom and saw James lying across the bed sound asleep. "Fuck it!" she said to herself as she quietly removed her .380 with the silencer already attached to the barrel, and aimed it at James's head. Angela held the gun pointed at James's head for about five minutes before she finally placed her gun back in its holster. "I'll save him for last," she told herself as James turned and woke up right at that very moment.

"Hey baby" James said as he stretched. "When did you get here?"

"Just now baby," Angela said as sat down on the edge of the bed. "How has your day been?"

"Good," James replied with a smile. "Finally able to get some much needed rest."

"You hungry?" Angela asked. She planned on relaxing with James for the night because tomorrow she was back to business.

# CHAPTER 15

Capo rapped along with Young Jeezy as he packed the remainder of his things for his vacation. After listening to Kim, Capo realized that he did need a vacation.

"On some real shit," Kim began. "I might not ever come back," she said, as she put her makeup on in the mirror. "I don't think you should come back either."

"I have to come back to go to court," Capo told her as he slid his .45 down in his waistband.

"You really think them crackers gonna let you get off this time around?" Kim said turning to face Capo. "Nigga you better wake the fuck up! They planted drugs in your car, regardless you going to have to do some time, and you know once they get you in there they going to make sure you never leave. Probably pay some clown to fuck with you and wait for you to shank him." Capo knew what Kim was saying was right, but what she was asking him to do was the hardest thing in the world. To ask a drug dealer to leave the game while still in his prime was like asking him to commit suicide. Right now, he was on top and planned on staying that way.

"Fuck it! I say we just leave and don't come back," Kim told him.

"Together we got about $200,000. I say we just leave and make that shit work."

"What about our empire?" Capo asked.

"Fuck that shit," Kim said waving her hand. "Leave that shit with Bone, and let him just send us our cut."

"You think he can handle that?" Capo asked not sure if he should leave everything he had worked so hard to get with Bone.

"He's going to have to, because if you come back then you might as well go turn yourself in right now," Kim told him.

"Fuck it! We can leave and try to open up a business or something," Capo said. "As long we getting money somehow then we can stay, deal?"

"Deal," Kim agreed happily, as she jumped up in Capo's arms. Just as the two were about to celebrate, Kim heard her cell phone ringing. She looked at the caller I.D. and saw her mother's name flashing across the screen. "Hey mommy," Kim sang happily into the receiver.

"Bitch do this sound like your motherfucking mother to you?" The voice on the other end barked.

"Who is this?" Kim asked. The caller now had her undivided attention.

"Shut the fuck up!" Dough Boy barked into the receiver. "If you want to see your mother again then pay attention, first off I'm going to need $150,000 cash, and secondly you must come alone when you bring the money I'll call you tonight with further details" Dough Boy said as he hung up in Kim's ear.

"Who the fuck was that?" Capo asked as soon as Kim closed her phone.

"They got my mother," Kim said as she slid down the wall so that her knees were press on her chest. "They are going to kill her!"

"Calm down," Capo said squatting down next to Kim. "Who has your mother?"

"I don't know" Kim cried. "But it sounded like that stickup kid, the big one."

"How much they want to give her back?" Capo asked.

"They want $150,000," Kim sobbed. Capo knew once he paid the ransom that he would never leave New York, and his life was now over, especially since the cops were now gunning for him, but there was no way he could let Kim's mother suffer because of some beef that they had in the streets. "We'll get your mother back, by any means" Capo assured her. "Don't even worry about it."

\*\*\*

"What's your name?" Dough Boy asked as he untied Kim's mother's hands. He didn't really want to hurt the woman, but if she didn't cooperate, he wouldn't hesitate to put her back in her place.

"Michelle," the woman replied in a shaky voice. Dough Boy could tell that the woman was scared to death. "Listen to me carefully," he said making sure Michelle understood what he was about to say. "I'm about to untie you, please don't try to run, because you won't be able to out run a bullet," Dough Boy said as he cut the tape from around her wrist. "Don't make me hurt you. All I want is the money."

"I'm not going to try and run," Michelle assured him. "So why are you doing this? Did my baby do something to hurt you?"

Dough Boy smiled as he cracked open the brand new bottle of Vodka that rested on the counter. "No your daughter didn't do anything to me."

"Then why are you doing this?" Michelle asked as she got up, grabbed herself a glass from out the cabinet, and held it out.

# SILK WHITE

"Honestly, I just really need the money," Dough Boy replied as he filled up Michelle's cup. He felt bad for what he was doing, but he had to do what he had to do. Dough Boy always walked in a situation planning just to rob his target, if he happened to shoot them or even murder them he looked at it as if it was their fault, because he only used his weapon if he had too.

"I hope you have a better reason for trying to rob an older woman, than just you need the money," Michelle said sipping from her glass. "You are putting a lot of lives in jeopardy pulling a move like this."

"My son is very sick, and if I don't get $100,000 he's going to die." Dough Boy told her as his eyes began to moisten. Every time he thought about his little man, he got emotional.

"I understand," Michelle said seeing the pain in Dough Boy's face when he spoke about his son. "I just hope everything works out for you and your family," a part of her wanted to feel sorry for Dough Boy. She could really feel his pain, but at the same time, he was going about getting money the wrong way, and she knew the kind of people her daughter hung out with, so she was sure that the outcome would end in a bloody mess.

# CHAPTER 16

"How long you going to be gone for?" James asked as he sat on bed and watched Angela jam her clothes in a suitcase.

"Two to three weeks tops" Angela assured him with a smile. "Sorry I have to go on such short notice, but my mom is really sick," she lied.

"I understand," James said. "Go handle your business." Angela hated to have to lie to James, but there was no way she could tell him that she wasn't going to see her mother, but instead going on a killing spree. Angela felt bad, but business was business.

"You need me to drop you off at the airport?" James asked.

"No that's alright," Angela quickly declined. "I'll just take a cab."

"You sure?" James pressed. He wanted to spend as much time with Angela as he could, especially since she was about to be leaving him.

"I'll be back in no time baby," Angela said as she kissed James on the lips as she heard the cab outside blowing its horn. She quickly grabbed her two bags, one, which held clothes inside, and the other that held any kind of weapon and body armor she could think of as she headed out the front door. "Motel 6 downtown," Angela said as she slid in the back seat of the cab. The cab driver shook his head and pulled off. For the entire ride, Angela looked at a wallet-sized picture of the D.A. Heather. When the cab pulled up in the Motel 6 parking lot, Angela paid the man, grabbed her bags, and headed to the office so she could pay for her room for two weeks in advance in cash. Angela stepped foot in her room and immediately plugged in her iPhone, sat her iPod on the top and turned up the volume as T.I.'s song "I'm Back" pumped through the speakers. Angela quickly stripped out of her business suit, and threw on a pair of black pants, and some all black, easy to run in comfortable combat boots, she then put on her custom made Teflon vest that was made just to fit her breast size, a tight fitting all-black long sleeve shirt went over the vest. Angela stood in front of the mirror and sat her blonde wig on top of her head, followed by her dark tinted shades. Angela walked over to her suitcase and removed two .380's with the silencers already attached, three extra clips, a sharp throwing knife, and wrist straps that looked like bracelets but were really knives. Angela slipped her fingers inside the black gloves as she exited her room, and headed down the street in search of a vehicle. She walked up on a nice low-key Honda, and with a flick of her wrist, a sharp blade sat in the palm of her hand. Once inside the car she quickly hotwired the car and was on her way to pay Heather a visit.

Angela parked her car two blocks away from Heather's house as she slid out the driver's seat and quietly walked through the woman's grass until she reached the front door. With the same knife that she broke into the car with she used to pick the lock on the front door. Once inside, Angel made sure she closed the door behind her quietly as she removed one of her .380's and held it with a two handed grip as she moved throughout the house as quiet as a cat as she searched for her target. She placed her back up against the wall as she heard some movement coming from upstairs. Angela quickly made her way up the steps until she reached the top of the steps. Upstairs were four bedrooms, but movement only in one. Angela slowly crept up on the door, and kicked it open. Inside she saw man standing with no shirt on.

"Who the hell are you?" The man asked. One shot to his head silenced him forever. Angela walked up to his body and pumped three more shots in his chest just for the hell of it. She then trained her gun on Heather the same woman from the picture. She sat in a rocking chair holding a baby in her arms that couldn't have been any older than six months old. Just as Heather fixed her mouth to scream, Angela put a bullet right between her eyes, causing Heather's head to lean forward as the blood from the hole in her head dripped on the little baby. Angela then trained her gun on the infant, and held it there for a second before sliding her weapon back in its holster. She walked over and removed the baby who was now screaming at the top of her lungs from Heather's arms, and placed her in her crib. Once Angela was sure the baby was safe, she turned and exited the house.

When Angela made it back to her room, she quickly removed all of her clothes and hopped straight in the shower where she stood for about an hour before she finally hopped out. Angela threw on a nightgown as she hopped in the bed and texted James. "Hey baby, I know you probably sleep just wanted to let you know that I made it to my mother's house safe and sound. I'll call you tomorrow. I love you, Muaaaaah," she typed before pressing the send button. Angela tossed her phone on the nightstand, and grabbed her iPod. She put on some Lauren Hill, and then pulled out a small picture of her next target Judge Michael Steward.

\*\*\*

Capo stood in his crib along with Kim, Bone, and about six other soldiers. He still couldn't believe this was happening on the day that he and Kim were supposed to be leaving. If it weren't for bad luck, Capo would have no luck at all.

"This motherfucker gotta die after pulling some shit like this," Bone spat pacing back and forth smoking a cigarette. "Motherfucker wants $150,000.00?"

"$150,000.00 cash" Kim repeated with a stone look on her face. She didn't care how much money Dough Boy wanted, all she cared about was getting her mother back safe and sound. "And he said I gotta come alone when I bring him the money."

"Fuck outta here!" Bone huffed. "I'm not letting you take that money to that nigga all by yourself, what if it's a set up?'

"We don't have any other options," Capo said. "He got the upper hand so we gotta play by his rules for now." Capo didn't want to send Kim alone carrying $150,000.00 but what other choices did he have?

"Fuck it!" Bone cursed loudly looking over at Capo. "I say me and you follow her, I mean how do we even know her mother is even still alive?" Before anyone could say another word, Kim's cell phone rang. The whole room got so quiet that one could hear a pin drop.

"That's him?" Capo asked looking at Kim for a response. She looked at the caller I.D. and shook her head yes, as she answered the phone. "Hello?"

"You got my money?" Dough Boy asked cutting straight to the chase.

"Yeah I got it," Kim replied. "But you not getting shit until I speak to my mother to make sure she's okay first." A long pause occurred then seconds later Kim heard her mother on the other end of the phone.

"Hello?"

"Mommy are you alright?" Kim asked happy to hear her mother's voice.

"Yes baby I'm fine" Michelle assured her.

"I'm on my way down there to get you," Kim said just as Dough Boy got back on the phone.

"Meet me downtown at Time Square in an hour in front of BB King's and if you don't come alone, your mother is dead," Dough Boy said hanging up in Kim's ear. Kim closed her phone and shook her head. "I'm going to have to go alone."

# THE TEFLON QUEEN

"Fuck!" Capo cursed as he walked up and handed Kim a brand new chrome 9mm. "If shit don't look right you know what to do. Bone and I are going to just follow you to make sure nothing happens to you."

"You sure that's a smart move?" Kim asked as she grabbed the duffle bag filled with the money.

"We are going to stay a few blocks behind you just to make sure you safe." Capo told her as she, Capo and Bone headed out the door.

\*\*\*

"Come on it's time to go," Dough Boy said removing his .45 from his waistband.

"You sure you want to go through with this?" Michelle asked making sure he knew exactly what he was about to get himself into.

"Positive," Dough Boy winked at her. He didn't want to do this, but instead he had to, nothing or no one came above or before his family. Dough Boy grabbed Michelle by her arm and led her outside to the car that waited curbside for them. The driver was a young kid named Dee who was just trying to make himself a couple dollars.

"Take us to forty deuce," Dough Boy order as he and Michelle slid in the back seat. Dee nodded his head, and quickly pulled off into traffic.

\*\*\*

Kim walked up to B.B. Kings and saw Dough Boy already standing there waiting on her with his hand on his hip. "You late," Dough Boy said as soon as Kim walked up.

"Where's my mother?" Kim said ignoring the comment he just made.

# SILK WHITE

"Is that my money?" Dough Boy said eyeing the duffle bag.

"Where's my mother?" Kim asked again. Dough Boy snatched the bag from her hand, then pulled out his cell phone and made a call. "Yeah everything is straight. Bring her mother," he said before shutting his phone. "Your mother will be here in two minutes," Dough Boy said as he turned and quickly disappeared down the subway steps.

"Fuck!" Kim cursed as she watched Dough Boy escape. Minutes later, Kim saw a burgundy car pull up and seconds later her mother hopped out the back. "My babbbby!" Michelle yelled as she and Kim hugged in the middle of the street.

"Follow that motherfucker!" Capo said pointing at the burgundy car. Bone nodded his head and quickly followed the burgundy car. After following the burgundy car around the city for about forty-five minutes, the car finally parked in front of a housing project. Dee hopped out the burgundy car feeling good. He had just made a quick $1,000 to do absolutely nothing, his life was just starting to turn around for the better, or so he thought. Just as Dee locked the door on his burgundy Buick, he turned around to a big ass gun in his face.

"Nigga get over here!" Capo snarled as he roughly grabbed Dee by the back of his shirt and roughly tossed him in the trunk. Once Capo got back in the car, Bone pulled off.

When the trunk popped open, Bone quickly snatched Dee from out of it. "Bring yo ass over here!" he said roughly forcing Dee through a door and into a room full of rough looking men.

"What's this all about?" Dee asked nervously.

"Sit down," Capo said in an even tone. From the look on his face, Dee could tell he wasn't in a good or happy mood. "Listen carefully motherfucker!" Capo began. "I'm only going to ask you this once, where the fuck is Dough Boy?"

"I don't know" Dee replied. Seconds later, he felt a bottle crashing over his head.

"This nigga must think we playing" Bone said as he snuffed Dee with all his might. Seconds later, Dee's eye went completely shut.

"You better tell me something," Capo said roughly grabbing Dee's chin.

"If you don't know where he's at, then you better tell us where we can find him."

"I don't know," Dee said as he closed his eyes preparing for what was coming next.

"Hold it!" Michelle yelled as she and Kim walked up in the spot. "I know where y'all can find him."

"Where?" Bone asked ready to put in some work. Michelle didn't really want to tell on Dough Boy, after spending time with the man she found out that he was just a regular man put in a bad situation, and she knew anybody put in the same predicament would have done the exact same thing. "You'll be able to find him at the hospital," Michelle said.

"His son is very sick with a heart problem that's what he needed the money for."

"I hope it was worth it." Bone huffed as him and a few goons headed straight for the hospital. As Capo readied to leave with Kim, and her mother he heard a goon yell. "Hey what you want us to do with this nigga?" Capo turned around and saw Dee sitting helplessly in the chair.

"Your call" he said as he headed for the door. Capo hadn't even made it two steps before he heard the goons beating the shit out of Dee. He shook his head and kept on walking.

\*\*\*

James stepped out of his car and saw police everywhere, from the looks of it, whatever had went down had to be bad. News vans and reporters covered the entire block. "F.B.I. coming through," James said flashing his badge as he squeezed through the crowd. He ducked under the yellow tape before being stopped by a detective. James quickly flashed his badge and the detective apologized. "What we got here?" James asked.

"Homicide," the detective replied. "A man and a woman both murdered at point black range."

"Any witnesses or leads?" James asked as he and the detective entered the house.

"None" the detective replied. "Neighbors say they saw a woman leaving the house late last night a blonde, but whoever did this was kind enough not to kill the little baby thank God."

James made it upstairs to the murder scene and immediately recognized Heather. "I know her," he said to the detective.

"She had any enemies?" the detective asked.

"Plenty" James replied. "She was a D.A." as James sat looking at Heather's dead body a thought quickly popped in his mind, he remembered when he used to work for Wayne he would always say if them pigs ever arrested him he would take his last money and put a hit out on the judge and the D.A. "Fuck!" James cursed loudly as he pulled out his cell phone and dialed up his boss's number. "Hello? Yeah it's me, James. I need the name of the judge that's been assigned to Wayne's case. I need that as soon as possible," he said ending the call. If Wayne was the one responsible for this murder, James knew he would have to act fast, because there was no telling when the judge would pop up missing. Thirty minutes later, James heard his cell phone ringing. "What you got for me?" He answered as he pulled out a pen, note pad, and scribbled down the info his boss was giving him on the other line. "I got it," James said ending the call. "I need a few of your men to follow me out to this location," he said looking at the detective. "If I'm right, that's where the killer will be striking next," he said as he and a few detectives rushed out the door and headed to the Judge Michael Steward's house.

# CHAPTER 17

Angela parked the stolen Ford Explorer a block away from her latest target Michael Steward's house. She quickly glanced in the mirror, and saw that her blonde wig sat perfectly on top of her head. Angela placed a black skullcap over her wig, and threw on her dark shades, as she hopped out the vehicle and made her way towards the front door. With a flick of her wrist, a blade magically appeared in the palm of her hand again as she quickly picked the lock. Once Angela got the door open, she quietly crept inside and shut the door behind her. Instantly, Angela's .380 with the silencer attached found itself in her hands as she quietly eased her way the house. Angela crept through the kitchen and saw Michael sitting in the living room with his back to her. She quietly walked up on the judge from behind and put three bullets in the back of his head. Angela then quickly searched the rest of the house just to make sure she and the judge were the only ones in the house alone. Once her work was done Angela quickly headed to the front door, but stopped dead in her tracks when she heard noises coming from outside. She looked through the peephole and about seven to eight white men holding guns heading straight for the front door. Angela swiftly ran in the kitchen and turned the gas on the stove on then hid behind the wall as she removed a small mirror from back pocket.

"Be careful," James said as he clutched his .45 tightly. "If our suspect is in there, he's considered armed and very dangerous," he said as they all entered the house one by one. Angela held her mirror out just enough so she could see exactly what the officers were doing. Angela eyes grew wide when she recognized James through the small mirror. "What the fuck is he doing here?" She thought. "Fuck it! It's either me or him," Angela told herself as she sprung from around the corner and fired five shots, each shot found a home in several of the officers bodies as she quickly dashed up the stairs. When James and the other officers saw the gunman make a dash for the steps they automatically opened fired causing the stove to explode. James quickly covered his face as the explosion blew him back out the front door. Angela ran up the stairs as fast as she could, but she wasn't fast enough, as the impact from the explosion managed to shoot her up the remainder of the steps tossing her into the wall. "Fuck!" Angela cursed as she picked up her .380 up from off the floor and slid it back into her holster as she entered the closest room and headed straight for the window. Angela lifted her leg and forcefully kicked through the glass as she crawled out to the roof of the house and jump down to the ground. Angela jumped from off the roof and landed on her feet. Before she could even take a step, she felt some cold steel pressed to the back of her head.

"Move and I'll blow your fucking head off!" James yelled. "Put them hands up so I can see them," he ordered with authority. Angela slowly put her hands up in the air, and in a quick motion she spun around and twisted James's wrist causing him to drop the gun dead in the palm of her hand. "I don't want to kill you," Angela said disguising her voice as she removed the clip from the base of the gun letting it drop to the ground; she then tossed the gun across the street. "You go your way and I'll go mine," she suggested. Once James saw the gunman that looked and spoke like a woman toss the gun across the street, he quickly made his move. James swung a wild haymaker trying to take off the gunman's head. Angela smoothly weaved the wild punch and landed a jab of her own. When she saw James remove his jacket and toss it on the ground, she knew it was time to go. "I don't have time to play with you!" Angela yelled removing her .380. "Get on the ground," Angela ordered. "Now!" she yelled as she watched James do as he was told. She quickly removed his handcuffs and cuffed his hands behind his back. Once she was sure that he wasn't going anywhere, she took off on foot as she heard sirens getting closer and closer. Angela ran back to the Ford Explorer and gunned the engine as she fled the crime scene.

James laid on the ground and heard one of the detective's exiting out of the house. "Over here!" He yelled. The detective quickly made his way over to James and uncuffed him. "Call for back up!" James yelled as he ran over to his Impala and stepped on the gas as he tried to catch up with the gunman.

# SILK WHITE

Angela weaved from lane to lane on the highway dodging traffic, while doing 90 mph. "I should have killed him," she told herself as she zipped by cars driving like a professional racecar driver. As Angela weaved from lane to lane, she noticed flashing lights in her rear view mirror. "Fuck!" She cursed as she pulled over to the side of the road. Angela watched the officer make his way over to the driver side of the truck through the rear view, and side mirrors. She rolled down the window as the officer tried to blind her with the bright ass light from his flash light. "How can I help you officer?" Angela asked politely.

"Ma'am, do you have any idea how fast you was going?" The officer asked as he looked inside the vehicle and saw a knife sticking out of the ignition. "Step out the car ma'am!" The officer said sternly. Angela slowly stepped out the truck and placed her hands on the hood of the Explorer.

"So you like stealing cars huh?" The officer asked as he began to search the sexy woman that stood in front of him. Once Angela felt the officer reach her two .380's, she quickly flicked her wrist, spun around and sliced the officer's throat. The officer quickly grabbed his throat with both hands as he gargled on his own blood while just staring at the woman who had just done this to him. Angela gave the officer a smirk as she saw a Mack truck flying down the highway. In a quick motion, Angela planted one foot on the ground and side kicked the officer out in the middle of the highway with her other foot. The Mack truck driver quickly stomped on his breaks, but it was a little too late as he watched the officer smack off the grill of his truck causing himself along with other vehicles to crash.

"Ooooh shit!" James yelled as he stomped on his brakes, as he saw several cars up ahead of him crash. When his car finally came to a complete stop, he saw the blonde hair gunman over on the side of the road. James quickly swerved his car around two cars as he road up on the shoulder of the road gunning straight at his target. Angela quickly pulled her .380 from her holster and sent five shots through James's front windshield causing him to duck down and crash into the back of the Ford Explorer.

James quickly hopped out the Impala with his .45 in hand, as he ducked down by the side of his vehicle. "It's on now motherfucker!" He yelled.

Angela looked over at the other side of the highway with cars flying in the other opposite direction, and made a dash for it.

"No fucking way," James said out loud, as he watched the gunwoman run over towards the other side of the highway. Angela ran full speed as she easily cleared the little rail that divided the two sides and landed on the other side immediately she heard tires screeching as cars quickly pumped their brakes when they saw a person running across the highway. Angela continued to run across the highway just as she was about to make it across to the other side she saw one car was late hitting the brakes. She quickly jumped up in the air and tucked her knees into her chest turning herself into a human ball as she felt the impact from the car as she rolled from the hood of the car, to the windshield, to the roof of the car, Angela hit the ground and landed on her back. She quickly hopped up and continued her get away on foot.

James looked on in amazement as he watched the gunwoman hop up from off the ground and take off running. He couldn't believe what he had just witnessed. James didn't know who this gunwoman was, but one thing he did know was whomever he or she was they were a professional, and he personally accepted the challenge to take the hit man down by any means necessary.

Angela jogged to the nearest red light, not wanting to look out of place. She saw a rich looking white woman stopped at the red light fishing through her purse not paying attention. Angela quickly walked up and snatched the woman out the car as if she was playing Grand Theft Auto. She hopped in the driver seat and peeled off leaving tire marks on the concrete.

# SILK WHITE

Angela stepped foot in her room and headed straight for the bathroom. She immediately filled the bath tub up half way with cold water, once that was done she grabbed her ice bucket and stepped out the room and filled it up with ice. Angela came back in the room and dumped the ice in the tub, stripped down butt naked and hopped in as she let the ice sooth her aching body as she rested her head on the back of the tub and closed her eyes.

*** 

The next day, James sat in his office behind his desk in deep thought. He couldn't and didn't understand why the gunwoman didn't pull the trigger when they had the drop on him.. Another thing he was certain of was that the gunman wasn't a man. Instead, she was a woman. Man or woman, it didn't matter. James was determined to catch whoever it was responsible for killing the D.A. and the Judge. As James sat behind his desk, he saw someone bust into his office. It was his boss Captain Jackson.

"What can you tell me about this hit man?" Captain Jackson asked dropping the daily news down on James's desk.

"Well first off, I don't think this hit man is a man" James began. "She is a woman and a highly trained woman at that," he said reading the head line on the front page of newspaper that read, "The hit man strikes again!"

"You think you can catch this fucker?" Captain Jackson asked. He knew James Carter was the best agent he had on his squad, and just hoped that his man would be able to catch this woman who was running around killing people as if it was nothing.

"I know I can" James replied confidently. "I always catch my man or woman in this case."

"Good" Captain Jackson said heading for the door. "Make it sooner than later please."

"Will do," James said as he watched his boss walk out of his office. He buried his face in his hands as he thought about how he was going to catch this killer. "I need to talk to my baby," James said as he pulled out his cell phone and dialed Angela's number.

***

Angela sat outside of James's office parked in a stolen car as she patiently sat, waiting for him to come out the building. She didn't want to kill James, but she knew if she didn't it would be just as if taking her own life because there was no way Mr. Biggz would allow her to keep her life if she broke a contract. "Fuck it gotta do what I gotta do," Angela told herself as she felt her cell phone vibrating. She looked at the caller I.D. and saw James' name flashing across the screen. "Hey baby," she answered happily. "I was just about to call you," she lied. "How's your day been so far?"

"Stressful," James began. "I almost got my head blown off last night."

"Are you serious baby?" Angela said pretending to be concerned. "You need me to come back home?"

"No baby I'll be fine," James told her. "I've just been assigned to this big case. I know you been watching the news."

"Yeah I saw it's some hit man killing people like it's going out of style." Angela said. "I hope that's not the case you've been assigned to."

"Yup that's the case" James replied. "But don't worry you know your man is the best."

# SILK WHITE

"I know you are daddy," Angela said fixing her blonde wig making sure it looked good on her before she placed her skullcap over it.

"Okay baby I love you, but I gotta go," James said.

"I love you too daddy," Angela said ending the call. She closed her phone and slid it in her pocket as she continued to wait patiently. While she waited, Angela loaded up her MP5 SMG automatic machine gun and sat it on her lap. About forty-five minutes later, Angela spotted James walking out of the building and headed towards his car.

James walked over to his car, hopped behind the wheel, and pulled off. Angela waited until James got about a mile away before she began to follow him. She made sure she stayed three cars behind him, waiting for the perfect opportunity to make her move as she sat her machine gun in the passenger seat. Angela kept her eye on her man the whole time. Part of her wanted to say 'fuck it' and just say forget the whole mission, but then the other half told her that if James was the one behind the trigger he wouldn't hesitate to pull it. "Fuck it!" Angela said out loud, as she snatched her .380 from her holster, held her arm out the window, and shot out the back tire on James car causing him to lose control of the vehicle.

"Oooooh shit!" James yelled as his car flipped over seven times and finally landing upside down.

Angela parked her car in the middle of the street, grabbed her machine gun from off the passenger seat, and hopped out the car. She walked up a few feet away from James car aimed the machine gun at the car and squeezed the trigger in broad daylight. The gun rattled in her hands as multiple shells popped out the gun until she ran out of bullets. Angela saw blood leaking from the side of James's head as she slowly began to back pedal back to her car, where she hopped behind the wheel and gunned the engine.

# CHAPTER 18

Dough Boy walked into the hospital carrying a duffle bag filled with $100,000 inside. He had finally got the money and couldn't wait to pay the doctor so his son could finally have the operation that he needed.

"Can I help you sir?" The lady behind the desk asked.

"Yes I'm looking for….Dr. Hill," Dough Boy said looking at the card.

"One second," the woman said as she picked up the phone, said a few words then hung it up. "He'll be down in one minute."

"Thanks," Dough Boy said politely as he paced back and forth in the lobby. Thoughts of his son raced through his mind as he continued to wait. The whole time Dough Boy kept his eyes open for any signs of trouble. After about a twenty minute wait, Dr. Hill finally made it down to the lobby.

"Hey Dr. Hill what's up?" Dough Boy said as he and the doctor shook hands.

"Pretty busy," Dr. Hill replied with a smile. "How can I help you?"

"I got the money so you can push my son's name up on the list for the heart surgery procedure," Dough Boy said, in a light whisper tapping the bottom of the duffle bag.

"Are you crazy?" Dr. Hill said in a stern whisper. "Don't you ever come up to my job with a bag full of cash. I gave you my card for a reason…use it," he said as he turned and walked off leaving Dough Boy standing there.

"Scary mufucka!" Dough Boy cursed. If he didn't need the doctor's help he would of definitely smacked the shit out of the white man for talking to him like that, but since Dr. Hill was the only that could help him at that very moment, Dough Boy had to eat his pride and hold that. Not knowing what else to do, Dough Boy grabbed his duffle bag and headed back out the way he had come in. Dough Boy stopped dead in his tracks when he looked up and saw Bone and a few other rough looking men leaning up against his car.

"Don't even think about trying to run" Bone said with his hand on his waist and a smirk on his face.

"I ain't gon run," Dough Boy announced. He cursed himself for leaving his gun in the car, but he was so busy rushing trying to hurry up and meet with the Dr. Hill that he left his gun on the floor of the car.

"What you got in the bag?" Bone asked as one of his goons walked up and snatched the duffle bag from his hands.

"Let's go ahead and get this over with," Dough Boy said as his eyes began to water. He felt like a failure and had let his son down in the process, and for that reason alone he no longer wanted to live on this earth anymore.

Bone just laughed as he watched his goons roughly toss Dough Boy in the van where they tied his hands together. A few goons were about to put hands on Dough Boy until Bone stopped them. "Save that for when we get to the spot," he told them.

\*\*\*

Capo sat on the couch sipping on some Cîroc as he looked at the disappointed look on Kim's face. "What's wrong with you?"

# THE TEFLON QUEEN

"My life is just all fucked up," Kim replied slamming her glass down to the floor. "All the work we put in over the years and what do we have to show for it? Nothing!" She said answering her own question. "Can't even go on a motherfucking vacation!"

"We gonna be fine," Capo said trying to calm her down. "We still got $50,000 saved up if you want to make moves with that you can."

"What we gon do with $50,000?" Kim huffed. "That ain't shit" they were so used to having so much money, that $50,000 to them was like $1,000. "Fuck this I quit," Kim said.

"Fuck you mean you quit?" Capo asked.

"I'm out the game, I don't want to do this shit no more," Kim said as she broke down into tears. All the hustling and killing had finally caught up to her after all these years. Kim had put in plenty of work for the crew, and knew that if she wanted out couldn't nobody tell her anything.

"So what you plan on doing for money?" Capo asked knowing once you were accustomed to fast money there was no way for one to go back to making regular money.

"I don't know," Kim said clearly frustrated.

"Oh shit!" Capo said, as he grabbed the remote and turned up the T.V. he couldn't believe his eyes.

"An eye witness captured this footage on her cell phone earlier today," The reporter said as Capo and Kim watched Angela shoot up someone's car in broad daylight. "Cops are still looking for the woman responsible at this time. The agent that was seriously wounded I'm just being told is James Carter. This has been Lisa Turner reporting live from Channel 2 News"

## SILK WHITE

"That bitch is crazy," Capo said as he saw Bone enter their hangout spot with a smile on his face. "I got a surprise for y'all," he sang. Seconds later, his goons brought Dough Boy through the door.

"That's what I'm talking about," Kim said as she ran over and punched Dough Boy in his face. "You thought we wasn't gonna find you?" Kim huffed as she punched him again taking out all her anger on him. Once the other goons saw Kim start to beat on Dough Boy, they quickly joined in. Dough Boy hit the floor and tried to cover his face as best he could as fist and feet came from every direction.

"That's enough," Capo said as he walked over to the man lying on the floor. "Get this nigga up!"

"And we got the money back too," Bone announced as he tossed the duffle bag in front of Capo's feet. Capo looked down at the duffle bag then back up at Dough Boy. "You just don't learn your lesson do you?" He asked pulling a knife from his back pocket.
"My son is very sick," Dough Boy said in an honest tone. "I need that money for him to get a heart transplant or else he's going to die."

"Nigga fuck your son!" Bone yelled as he snuffed Dough Boy. "You taking food from our kids mouth and you want us to feel sorry for your bitch ass son?" Capo quickly hushed Bone with a lift of his hand.

"If you needed help, all you had to do was come and ask for help," Capo told him. "You don't go and just take shit, especially from me or one of mine," Capo said as he slowly raised the knifed and plunged it in and out of Dough Boy's neck at least twenty times before he dropped the knife on the floor. Capo dug in Dough Boy's back pocket, and removed his wallet. "Get this clown up outta here!"

Capo picked the duffle bag from off the floor and headed for the door. "I'll holla at y'all later."

"Yo, what's up with this nigga?" Bone said as soon as Capo had left.

"This nigga been acting like a little bitch lately."

"He just got a lot going on right now," Kim said defending Capo. She knew why Capo had just began to slow down a bit, but she knew Bone would never understand.

"Fuck that!" Bone said loudly. "I'mma tell that nigga straight up if he ain't built for this shit no more then he needs to just pass this shit over to me."

Capo sat in his B.M.W, removed Dough Boy's I.D. from his wallet, and headed straight for the man's house. For the entire ride, Capo thought about what his next move would be. He thought about what Kim said about just leaving the game alone, but the thought of eventually going broke made him quickly erase that thought from his mind. Capo pulled up in front of Dough Boy's house and left the car running as he grabbed the duffle bag from off the front seat, and headed for the front door. Capo knocked on the door and patiently waited for an answer. Seconds later, Monica answered the door. "Hi can I help you?"

"Yeah Dough Boy told me to give this to you," Capo said handing her the duffle bag.

"Do you know where he's at I've been calling him and he's not answering his phone," Monica said taking the bag from Capo's hands.

"He's dead," Capo said as he turned and walked off. He tried to drown out the woman's cries as he hopped back in his B.M.W and peeled off.

Capo didn't have a destination. He just drove in deep thought. Capo pulled up to a red right and saw a strip club on the next corner. "Fuck it," he said as he pulled into the strip club's parking lot. Capo placed his .45 under his seat as he hopped out the whip and headed towards the front door. After being frisked by the bouncer, Capo enter the strip club. As soon as he stepped foot in the joint the saw ass everywhere as the beautiful strippers shook and moved their bodies to the sound of Gucci Mane blasting through the speakers. Capo made his way straight to the bar and ordered a bottle of Rosay, traded in three hundred dollar bills for three hundred singles, then headed over and took a seat over in the corner on the couch. Capo turned the bottle up and guzzled for about six seconds before turning the bottle back down. As soon as he sat his bottle down, he saw a redbone stripper standing directly in front of him with her back to him, she looked back at him as she made her ass bounce and jiggle without even moving.

"That's what the fuck I'm talking about," Capo said as he tossed a hand full of dollars at the woman. Once the stripper saw that Capo was spending money she really gave him the business. Redbone sat on Capo's dick and began grinding hard on him the whole time looking back at him. Capo leaned back and watched as the stripper worked her magic. "Yo what's your name?" Capo asked.

"Honey Bunz," she said as she leaned down and whispered in his ear as she continued to grind on Capo. She could tell by the look on his face that if they weren't in the crowded club that he would have had her bent over giving her what she needed.

"What you doing when you get off?" Capo asked licking his lips.

"You tell me," Honey Bunz countered. "I'm down for whatever," she knew exactly who Capo was. She had seen him around a few times. She just didn't know how to approach him at the time.

"I'm tryna get up with you," Capo said with confidence all in his voice.

"Cool," Honey Bunz.

## THE TEFLON QUEEN

"Let me finish getting this money and once I'm done we can be out."

"Go get ya money ma," Capo said as he watched Honey Bunz strut over towards some John and sit on his lap. Capo loved a woman that knew how to make money. Something about that just turned him on. Capo bobbed his head to the music as he sipped from his bottle, and watched the thick dark skin woman work the pole. As Capo sat chilling, he looked over in the cut and couldn't believe his eyes. "I know that's not who I think it is" he said to himself as he got up and headed over in that direction. Capo smacked a few of the stripper's asses as he made his way over to the other side of the club. A smile appeared on Capo's face when he walked up to the woman that sat on the couch sipping on some wine with her legs crossed. "Fuck you doing up in a spot like this?"

Angela looked up with an angry look her face, guys had been trying to hit on her all night with corny lines, so she thought it was someone else trying to get in her panties, until she looked up and saw Capo standing over her. "Hey what's up Capo?" Angela said with a smile.

"Fuck you doing up in here?" Capo asked sitting down next to her. When they both worked for Wayne the two didn't get along, but they always respected one another.

"Just needed a spot to just come and clear my head" Angela replied. "I got a lot on my mind right now."

"I know," Capo said, taking a swig from his bottle. "I saw you on the news earlier."

Angela smirked. She knew only people that she did business with would recognize her or be able to identify her. To the rest of the world she was still a mystery and that's just how she planned to keep it. "Yeah you already know how I do."

"Just be careful," Capo told her. "Half the cops in this world are out looking for you right now."

"Let em look," Angela said pouring herself another glass of wine. The last thing on her mind was the police capturing her. The thing that was on the front of her mind was James and his condition. She did what she had to do, but the man she loved still rested heavy on her brain. "So what you been up too?" She asked quickly changing the subject.

"I've been good you already know still getting this money," Capo said watching the different naked women walk back and forth.

"Be careful out here," Angela warned. "You know that nigga Crazy Moe was the one that set Wayne up, so ain't no telling if he dragged your name in mix as well."

"I know," Capo said as Honey Bunz walked up and whispered in his ear.

"Going to get dressed, give me about fifteen minutes," she said. Capo nodded his head as he smacked her ass as she turn and walked towards the dressing room. "You just make sure you be careful out here."

"I got this," Angela said with a smile as the two shook hands.

Capo stood up when he saw Honey Bunz exit the dressing room looking even better than she did when she went in.

"So where we headed?" Capo asked when he and Honey Bunz made it outside the club.

"We can just go to my crib," Honey Bunz suggested. "You cool with that?"

"Let's do it," Capo said as he hopped in his B.M.W and waited for Honey Bunz to go get her car. Seconds later, she pulled up next to him in an all-black Lexus. "Follow me!" Honey Bunz yelled from the window as she pulled off. For the entire ride all Capo could think about was how good the sex between him and Honey Bunz was going to be. He followed her to a nice sized house. "She getting money," Capo thought to himself as he parked his B.M.W right behind her Lexus.

"Well this is it," Honey Bunz announced as the two entered her house.

"You doing good for yourself," Capo said as he flopped down on her leather couch.

"Hold on, you have to take off your shoes" Honey Bunz said, as she removed her heels and let her feet sink into her thick plush carpet.

"So let me guess you just dancing so you can pay for school right?" Capo asked as he removed his Prada shoes.

"School?" Honey Bunz repeated looking at Capo as if he was insane. "I don't give a fuck about no school, I dance to get paid."

"So is dancing all you do?" Capo asked walking around the house as if it wasn't his first time there.

"No that's not all I do," Honey Bunz said popping her Lil Wayne mix tape in her system.

"So what you a prostitute?" Capo asked helping himself to some juice.

"A prostitute?" Honey Bunz echoed. "Nah you got me fucked up, I ain't never sold my pussy," she said in a serious tone. "But I do what I gotta do."

"Oh word?" Capo asked with a smile on his face.

"Been doing it for the past three years," Honey Bunz said proudly.

She figured if the girls at the club was going to fuck anyway then she might as well make some money off it.

"I definitely ain't mad at that," Capo said. "Get that money."

"I take care of myself, and as you can see I like the finer things in life, so I gotta do what I gotta do point blank," Honey Bunz said. "I'm going to go hop in the shower. Make yourself at home," she said as she disappeared upstairs. Capo sat bobbing his head to the music as he waited for Honey Bunz to return from her shower. Suddenly, he heard a loud knock at the door. BAM, BAM, BAM! Seconds later the knocks got louder. BAM, BAM, BAM!

"Who the fuck is banging on the motherfucking door like that?" Capo said out loud, as he got up off the couch and headed over to the door. He looked through the peephole and saw a man standing on the other side of the door.

"Fuck is you knocking on the door like the motherfucking police for?"" Capo asked with an irritated look on his face. The man that stood on the other side of the door looked like he had been working out since the day he was born.

"Who the fuck are you?" The big man asked looking Capo up and down as if he was ready to snap his neck.

"What do you want?" Capo asked.

"I asked you a question," the big man repeated in a stern voice. Capo sighed loudly as he reached for his waistband, before he got a chance to pull out his strap he heard Honey Bunz voice.

"Mike, what are you doing here?" Honey Bunz asked coming to the door wearing nothing but a silk robe wrapped around her body.

"Who the fuck is this clown?" Mike asked still staring Capo down.

"What are you doing here?" Honey Bunz said grabbing Mike's chin so he could focus on her.

"I got something for you. Did you forget?" Mike told her.

"Oh shit my bad, go get that for me," Honey Bunz said as she watched Mike head back to his car. Mike was originally from New York, but had moved out to Atlanta so he could sell his coke for more money. Money Mike is what the streets called him. "Sorry about that he's just my supplier," Honey Bunz said as she ran upstairs and returned carrying a book bag. Money Mike returned carrying a book bag of his own.

"So you gon give it to me or not?" Honey Bunz asked placing one hand on her hip.

"I don't know this nigga," Money Mike said looking over at Capo who was sitting on the couch. "Look like a cop if you ask me," he said as he and Honey Bunz stepped over into the kitchen.

"Who the fuck is this nigga?" Money Mike asked in a light whisper.

"My friend," Honey Bunz replied. "And I don't appreciate you coming in here disrespecting my company."

"Y'all fucking?" Money Mike asked with a hint of jealousy in his voice. Back in the day, he and Honey Bunz used to be an item, but once Honey Bunz caught him cheating she put an end to their relationship.

"That's none of your business and if I want to fuck him then I will." Honey Bunz said as the two traded bags. She then escorted him to the door. Money Mike made sure he grilled Capo before finally leaving.

"Sorry about that," Honey Bunz apologized once Money Mike was gone.

"Well I didn't want to tell you all of my business, but I also sell a little coke on the side," she said tossing the book bag on the counter.

"Get that money," was all Capo said as he leaned back on the couch. Honey Bunz smiled at Capo's last comment as she lit a few candles and turned out the lights. She then switched the music from Lil Wayne to Erykah Badu. Honey Bunz stood directly in front of Capo and dropped her robe.

"Damn," Capo said trying to play it cool.

"Do you mind doing me a favor?" Honey Bunz asked in a sexually charged voice as she removed the rubber band from her long ponytail.

"Depends," Capo said licking his lips. Honey Bunz walked over to the counter and grabbed a bottle of baby oil then walked back over to where Capo sat. "Can you help me rub this oil in?" She said as she began to pour oil all over her body making it glisten. Capo quickly sat up and removed his shirt, as he began rubbing the oil all over Honey Bunz's voluptuous body. Once Capo finished rubbing baby oil all over Honey Bunz's body, she stepped up on the couch looking down at Capo. "Come eat this motherfucking pussy," she demanded as she tossed Capo down on the couch, and began to ride his face. "Oh shit," Honey Bunz whispered when she felt Capo began to work his tongue beneath her. "That's right eat this pussy," Honey Bunz moaned loudly as she gripped his head tightly and moved her buttocks in a circular motion, gyrating in his face until she felt herself releasing. Honey Bunz quickly hopped up and removed Capo's pants. She removed his gun from his waist and sat it on the coffee table, then finished removing the rest of Capo's clothes. A smile came to her face when she saw Capo's equipment standing at attention. Honey Bunz grabbed Capo's pole and slowly slipped him in her mouth, humming and moaning like an animal. Capo groaned as he grabbed the back of Honey Bunz's head with two hands and began to fuck her mouth like it was a pussy. Honey Bunz moaned loudly with each stroke that Capo delivered to her mouth until he filled her mouth. Honey Bunz made sure she swallowed every drop as she continued to kiss and lick Capo's pipe until it was standing back up at attention. Capo grabbed his jeans from off the floor and removed a condom from his pocket. Honey Bunz took the condom from his hand, opened it, and put it in her mouth. She took Capo deep into her mouth and when she removed her mouth, his condom was on. Honey Bunz then stood up and bent over leaning on the arm of the couch.

"Come get this pussy," she purred. Capo didn't waste any time positioning himself behind Honey Bunz.

"Damn," he said once he entered her tight walls, she was so wet that it felt like he wasn't even wearing a condom at all. With each stroke Capo delivered Honey Bunz made she threw her ass back at him, loving how he filled her up. "Shit!" Capo groaned as he spread both of Honey Bunz ass cheeks apart as he watched himself slide in and out of her, with each stroke he went deeper and deeper. Once Capo felt himself about to cum, he sped up his strokes. He watched Honey Bunz's ass jiggle and bounce up against his torso until he finally couldn't take it no more. "Ahggg!" Capo yelled as he exploded, then collapsed on to the carpet. "Damn" he huffed. "You don't be playin.g"

"I ain't got time to play," Honey Bunz countered. "Come to the bathroom so I can clean you off," she yelled over her shoulder as she headed to the bathroom. Capo peeled himself up off the carpet, went to the bathroom got cleaned off and headed straight for the bedroom where the two went and crashed for the rest of the night.

# SILK WHITE

The next morning, Capo woke up to someone knocking at Honey Bunz's front door. "Who the fuck is that?" Capo asked quickly grabbing his .45 from off the nightstand.

"Relax," Honey Bunz said as she hopped up and threw on her robe. "Just one of my customers."

Capo hopped up and got dressed while Honey Bunz went and took care of her customer, the fact that she was a straight up hustler made Capo like her even more.

"Where are you going?" Honey Bunz asked once she stepped back in the room and saw Capo fully dressed.

"Gotta go take care of some business myself," Capo told her. "But I'll definitely be back later," he promised. "You gotta work tonight?"

"Yeah," Honey Bunz replied.

"A'ight, holla at me when you get off," Capo said, as he kissed her on the cheek and then headed out the door.

***

Capo pulled up in front of the building in which he was looking for, and turned off his car off. He ran up three flights of stairs and knocked on the door he was looking for. "I hope she home," Capo thought as he knocked again. Seconds later, Ms. Pat swung the door open.

"Hello miss, is Shekia home?" Capo asked politely.

"Don't you ever come knocking on my door again you hear me?" Ms. Pat said in a stern motherly voice. She hadn't forgotten about the bottle that Capo had busted over her head, and the fact that he had murdered someone in her home, and now that her daughter was now hanging out with drug dealers and murderers made her even more upset. "You are not welcomed here!"

"Sorry to bother you ma'am," Capo apologized. "But can I speak speak to Shekia for a second?"

"Motherfucker!" Ms. Pat began. "Didn't I just say you weren't welcomed here?" Before Capo could say anything else, Shekia came from out the back room wondering what all the commotion was.

"Mommy what are you doing?" Shekia yelled as she rushed to the door.

"No!" Ms. Pat yelled. "I won't let you destroy your life any longer!"

Capo sat and watched as Shekia and her mother tussled at the door for what was only a few seconds, but seemed like forever.

"I am grown," Shekia yelled.

"Well if you grow then get the fuck out and don't ever come back!" Ms. Pat yelled as she shoved Shekia out into the hallway with Capo and slammed the door behind her.

"Stupid bitch!" Shekia cursed as she kicked the door. She hated how her mother acted and treated her like a baby.

"Sorry about that," Capo apologized. "I didn't mean to get you kicked out."

"It's not your fault," she said. "She been acting up ever since I started working with you" Shekia told him. "And I'm sick of her and her shit."

"I was just coming to tell you that I need you to make another trip for me," Capo said. "But I know how you and Scarface feel about one another so after this last one, your free to do as you please."

"For real!" Shekia said as her eyes lit up.

"Word," Capo told her. He knew that she no longer wanted to be here in New York, besides she had already put in more than enough work for him.

"When do you need me to make the trip?" Shekia asked.

"Tonight," Capo replied. "Can you handle that?"

"Definitely," Shekia replied.

# CHAPTER 19

Angela laid on her motel bed wearing nothing but a thong with her hands behind her head staring up at the ceiling. The only thing on her mind was James, this is the exact reason why she didn't do relationships, in the business she was in there were no room for emotions, or feelings, and now Angela was finding that out the hard way. She kept herself isolated from the rest of the world, as she laid low in her motel room. She kept trying to tell herself that it was just business, but her heart wasn't trying to hear that. Angela continued to stare up at the ceiling until she heard her cell phone ring. She looked at her phone and saw Mr. Goldberg's name flashing across the screen. "Hey what's up?" She answered.

"Hey Angela are you busy at the moment?" Mr. Goldberg asked.

"Not at the moment why what's up?" She asked.

"I need you to swing by my office as soon as possible."

"I'm on my way," Angela said ending the call. She hopped up took off her thong and hopped in the shower. Angela hopped out of the shower and quickly got dress and headed out the door. She hopped in her Lamborghini and headed straight for Mr. Goldberg's office. Angela pulled up in the empty parking spot and immediately the suicide door rose, as she stepped out and headed in the building. Angela's heels clicked loudly against the floor as she made her way to the lady that sat behind the desk. "How you doing, my name is Angela, and Mr. Goldberg is expecting me," she said in a polite manner.

"Yes he's right in his office," the woman replied as she watched Angela head back to Mr. Goldberg's office.

# SILK WHITE

Angela stepped foot in the office and saw Mr. Goldberg sitting behind his desk talking on the phone. "Yeah she just walked in hold on," he said as he handed the phone to Angela. "Hello?" She said once she placed the phone to her ear.

"Number 2?" The voice on the other end of phone said. Instantly, Angela knew it was Mr. Biggz on the other end of the phone. He always called her number 2 because he told her she was the second best assassin in the world.

"Yeah it's me," Angela replied.

"James Carter survived your hit," Mr. Briggz told her. "Is everything alright? Cause it's not like you to miss a hit"

"Everything is fine," Angela replied.

"Okay well I need you to go make that right," he said. Seconds later, the line went dead. Angela handed Mr. Goldberg back the phone.

"Are you alright?" He asked her.

"Yes I'm fine," Angela told him. She couldn't believe what she was just told. James was still alive.

"Well here's the address to the hospital were that bitch ass agent is being held. Can you believe he even snitched on me?" Mr. Goldberg said heated. "Please make sure you get rid of him this time," he said as he handed her the paper with the hospital's address on it.

"I'll take care of it," Angela said as she hopped up and exited Mr. Goldberg's office. Once she got outside, a big smile appeared across her face as she removed her heels and ran to her car and peeled out of the parking lot like a bat out of hell headed to the hospital.

# THE TEFLON QUEEN

Angela ran up in the hospital and headed straight for the woman who was on the phone that stood behind the desk. "Excuse me," Angela said out of breath. The woman spoke on the phone for about thirty more second before she hung up. "How can I help you?" She asked.

"James Carter," Angela said. "Can you please tell me what room he's in?" The woman searched through her computer, then looked up.

"Room 504"

"Thank you so much" Angela said thankfully, as she hurried over to the elevator. She hopped off the elevator and saw several cops standing in front of a room immediately she knew that was James' room.

"Can I help you ma'am?" An officer asked.

"Yeah I'm here to see my man," Angela said as she made it to the doorway of the room before the officer grabbed her. "Excuse me ma'am no one's allowed pass this point."

Once James looked up and saw Angela, he yelled. "Let her in!"

"Get off of me," Angela said snatching her arm from the officer's grip. When she stepped in the room, she saw James sitting on his bed along with a few other agents gathered around a computer. When Angela got close to James, she saw that he and the other agents were watching the video of her shooting up James's car.

"Oh my god baby I thought you were dead," Angela cried as she hugged him tightly.

"Takes more than a few bullets to kill me," James said cockily.

"Where did you get shot at baby?" Angela asked as she looked at James and he appeared to be fine.

"I only took one shot to my leg" James answered her.

"But how?" Angela asked. "I saw on the news that the gunman fired at least fifty rounds."

"Yeah but I knew she was coming so I was prepared," James told her.

"My body armor took twelve bullets and saved my life."

"Thank God that you are alive," Angela said in a worried voice.

"I'm fine baby," James told her. "But we are close to finding out who this gun lady really is and when we do her ass is mine!"

"You need me to do anything for you baby?" Angela asked.

"No baby I'm fine" James replied. He had his mind set on finding out who this gun lady was. Even if it was the last thing he did, he just had to take her down.

"Okay baby, is it okay if I stay here with you until your leg recovers?" Angela asked.

"Of course you can stay baby of course you can," James replied as he and the other agents continued to look at the video repeatedly.

\*\*\*

Cash walked through the yard with a mean look on his face. Inside he felt like shit, he had just found out that his main man Dough Boy had just been murdered, and there was nothing he could do about it because he was locked up. Cash didn't know how, but somehow he was going to kill Capo if he ever got the chance. "I gotta get the fuck up outta here," Cash said out loud, as he just continued to walk the yard.

"What's good fam?" A tough looking man wearing a du-rag yelled.

"Come get it in with us," he said as he and a group of men were doing pull-ups on the pull up bar.

"Nah I'm good," Cash said turning down the offer. As he continued to walk, he heard someone calling his name. When he looked up, he saw Wayne leaned up against the wall.

"Nigga what's good?" Cash said as he walked up and gave Wayne dap.

"Maintaining," Wayne replied with a smile. "What you doing up in here?"

"Got caught up in some shit," Cash said shaking his head in disgust.

"Yeah I heard you and Capo was going at it," Wayne said looking around. "But fuck all that. You want to make some money while you in here?"

"What I gotta do?" Cash asked knowing he was going to be down for a while, and wouldn't be getting out no time soon.

"I got a little something popping off in here," Wayne told him. "All I need you to do is look after my workers and make sure nobody don't try and take advantage of them."

"I think I can handle that," Cash said with a smirk on his face.

"Good," Wayne replied. "Now let's get this money," he said as the two shook hands.

# CHAPTER 20

Shekia stepped out of the airport and a huge smile came across her face when she saw Scarface's Range Rover waiting curbside for her.

"Hey baby," Shekia sang as she slid in the passenger seat and kissed Scarface on the lips.

"Glad you finally decided to come back and see me," Scarface said as he pulled away from the curb.

"Sorry baby, but you know I be having to take care of my business first." Shekia told him. "But after this trip, I'm done."

"No bullshit?" Scarface asked keeping his eyes on the road as he switched lanes.

"No bullshit," Shekia repeated with a smile. She knew that Scarface would be happy to hear the news.

"So," Scarface began. "Have you been thinking about what we talked about the last time you was here?" He asked as he alternated looking at the road and then back at Shekia.

"I thought about it," Shekia said as she turned in her seat so she could face him. "Are you really serious about me, because I don't want to move here then two, three months later you start acting brand new." Shekia knew a man like Scarface had to have a flock of woman waiting around somewhere, and she didn't want to move all the way out to Miami just to get hurt. Scarface immediately pulled over to the side of the road after that last comment.

# THE TEFLON QUEEN

"Let me tell you something" Scarface said. "I don't have time to play games. Life is too short for games. All I want to do is be happy, and you," he said pointing to her, "Makes me happy!"

Shekia smiled from ear to ear as she grabbed Scarface's face and gave him a sloppy kiss as the two started making out right in the car. Scarface lifted up Shekia's shirt and slipped one of her pretty perfect sized breast in his mouth as he licked and sucked all over her hardened nipples loving how they tasted. As Scarface sucked on Shekia's breast he slipped, his hands down to her stretch pants and slipped his hand down until he felt her magic button. Shekia let out light moans as Scarface played and massaged her clit with his hand. She even spread her legs open wider so he could be in a better position to make her cum. Shekia moaned loudly as she grinded her hip further on Scarface's hand as she leaned over, unzipped his shorts, and buried her face in between his legs giving him the best head in his life.

"Yeah just like that baby," Scarface instructed as he guided the back of Shekia's head with his hand making sure she was going at the perfect speed. Just when Scarface himself getting ready to cum, heard a loud knock at his window.

"What the fuck!" Scarface huffed as he looked up and saw a police officer shining a bright light looking at him and Shekia get busy. Scarface and Shekia looked at each other, then busted out laughing as they began fixing their clothes before stepping out of the car where they both were arrested and taken downtown to the police station.

*** 

"He ain't say that," Capo said getting angrier and angrier the more, and more he heard.

"Nigga said you turned soft, and he going to step to you about taking over the whole operation," Kim said relaying the message that Bone had told her.

"You know where that nigga's at right now?" Capo asked taking a sip from the foam cup he held in his hand filled with liquor.

"I know exactly where he's at," Kim said with a smirk on her face. She was tired of Bone talking shit as if he was the man, when really he didn't know shit about shit. Twenty minutes later, Kim doubled parked in front of the projects. Capo looked out the window and saw Bone standing in front of the building along with about fifteen other men.

"You want me to come with you?" Kim asked as she pulled out her .380 and sat it on her lap.

"Nah, I got this," Capo said as he hopped out the whip, and headed towards the building.

Bone stood in front of the building loud talking with the rest of his entourage when he saw Capo walking up. "Look at this nigga," he said as he and his crew laughed loudly.

"What's all this talk I been hearing about you about to take shit over, and all this other nonsense?" Capo said getting straight to the point and up close in Bone's face.

"I'm just saying" Bone began. "You been on some bullshit, acting like a bitch lately," he said. "If you ain't built for this shit no more then just say so, so I can run this shit the right way, the way it's supposed to be ran." As soon as those words left Bone's mouth Capo was already in motion. He caught Bone with a quick two-piece dropping the young man off impact. Capo quickly hopped on top of Bone and began pounding on his exposed face, until Bone was a bloody mess.

"Yo that's enough!" One of Bone's homeboys said as he grabbed Capo's shoulder trying to get him up off of his friend. Capo looked up with fire dancing in his eyes. He quickly pulled his .45 from his waist and fired two shots into the man's chest. Once the man's body dropped,

THE TEFLON QUEEN

Capo quickly ran back over to the car. As soon as he closed the door, Kim stomped on the gas pedal burning rubber as they left the crime scene in a hurry.

"You alright?" Kim asked as she zipped through traffic peeking through the rear view mirror.

"Yeah I'm good" Capo replied as he wiped his prints off the gun and tossed it out the window. "Tired of playing with these lil niggaz," he huffed.

"You should have let me handle that for you," Kim said knowing that was something he had to handle by himself.

"I'll be alright," Capo said. "I'mma just lay low for while....fuck it!"

"Where are you going to stay?" Kim asked.

"I don't know," Capo replied. "Just drop me off at that strip club down the block."

Kim pulled up in the strip club's parking lot, and placed the car in park. "So now what?"

"We just going to lay low, and wait it out for a little while," Capo suggested as he gave Kim a tight hug followed by a kiss. He was mad that Bone had forced his hand like that, but he had to do what he had to do. "Stay low," Capo said as he slid out the passenger side of the car, and headed towards the entrance of the strip club. Once Kim made sure Capo was in the club safe, she pulled off.

"Fuck!" Kim cursed as she pulled back out into the street she didn't know what it was, but for some reason, she felt like that was the last time she would ever see Capo again.

# SILK WHITE

Capo stepped in the strip club and headed straight for the bar, after the kind of day he had, he needed a drink bad. "Yo lemme get a bottle of Rosay!" He yelled over the music. Seconds later, the bartender handed Capo his bottle. "Damn!" Capo said as a sexy chocolate woman walked past him naked. "Damn, I might need to get up on that," Capo thought as he felt someone grab his shoulder. He turned around ready for action, until he saw Honey Bunz standing there.

"Damn baby you alright?" She asked with a smile. "Look like you was about to knock me the fuck out."

"Never baby" Capo said returning her smile as he gave her a big hug.

"What time you get off?"

"In about an hour" Honey Bunz replied. "Why, you need to be entertained for an hour?" She asked as she began to sway her hips from side to side in front of him.

"Save that for later baby, and go get that money," Capo said as he smacked Honey Bunz ass as he watched her walk over towards the pole. Capo sat back and watched as Honey Bunz worked the pole like a professional. Over by the entrance, he saw Money Mike enter the spot with a few of his homeboys. "Clowns," Capo said under his breath as he continued to watch the show that Honey Bunz was putting on. He watched as the other men in the strip club went crazy as they tossed all their hard-earned money at Honey Bunz. Just as Capo put his bottle up to his lips, he felt somebody bump into him causing him to spill Rosay on his shirt. Capo looked up and saw Money Mike standing there with a smirk on his face. Capo quickly swung the bottle with all his might as he smacked Money Mike across the face with the bottle causing shattered glass to spray everywhere. Before Capo got a chance to follow up, one of Money Mike's homeboys had punched him in the side of his head from behind causing him to stumble into another fist. Once Capo saw that he was outnumbered, he dropped his head and got his brawl on two on one. Money Mike finally got up off the floor holding his bloody eye. The first thing he did when he made it to his feet was pull his 9mm from his waistband and fired at whoever was in his way. The entire club went into a frenzy trying to run and duck and run for cover. Capo quickly scrambled towards the exit as he ran in a low hunch trying not to get hit with a stray bullet. As he ran towards the exit, he saw Honey Bunz searching for him through the crowd. "Come on let's go!" Capo yelled as he grabbed Honey Bunz by her arm, and rushed her up out the club. Honey Bunz ran as fast as she could in heels. When the two finally made it outside, Honey Bunz quickly kicked off her heels and ran through the parking lot barefoot with nothing on but a thong and her purse in her hand until they reached her Lexus. Honey Bunz hopped behind the wheel and burnt rubber as her Lexus swerved out the parking lot, out into the street.

"What happened back there?" Honey Bunz asked with a calm look on her face. After what just went down Capo expected her to be a nervous wreck, but instead she was as cool as a fan.

"That clown Money Mike came up there acting up so I had to spank his boots," Capo said as if it was no big deal. "He lucky I didn't have my bitch with me," he said referring to his .45.

"Damn!" Honey Bunz cursed. "That nigga better not bring that drama to my motherfucking house!"

"You got a ratchet in your crib?" Capo asked.

"Of course I do," Honey Bunz said looking at Capo like he was insane. As she pulled into her driveway, Capo watched as Honey Bunz walked up to the front door barefoot, wearing nothing but a pink thong.

"Yo lemme me get that strap just in case that clown try to make a movie later," Capo said as soon as he stepped foot in the house.

# SILK WHITE

"I got you baby," Honey Bunz said as she rushed upstairs. Two minutes later, she returned carrying a chrome 9mm.

"Here" Honey Bunz said as she handed him the gun. "It's already loaded and everything."

"Good looking," Capo said checking the clip himself just to make sure.

"I'll be right back I'm going to take a shower," Honey Bunz said as she headed for the bathroom. "The bottom of my feet are filthy from all that running." Capo watched as Honey Bunz ass jiggled with each step she took up the steps.

Capo waited for about five minutes before he followed her upstairs to the bathroom. He quickly removed all of his clothes before quietly entering the bathroom. Capo sat the 9mm on the top of the toilet as he slowly pulled the shower curtain back.

"I was wondering what was taking you so damn long," Honey Bunz said as she grabbed Capo by the waist and pulled him in the shower along with her. Once Capo was in the shower he watched as Honey Bunz melted down to her knees and take his erect member into her warm mouth and wrapped her juicy lips around his shaft. Her head bobbed up and down thoroughly lubricating Capo's dick. Honey Bunz slowly licked on the head of Capo's dick before sliding down to his ball and back up again.

"Bring ya sexy ass over here!" Capo demanded as he turned Honey Bunz around and made her grab the wall. He entered her behind slowly enjoying the feeling. Capo slid in and out her from behind nice and slow as he watched water splash off her ass. Just as Honey Bunz felt herself getting ready to cum she heard the bathroom door bust open. "FREEZE F.B.I DON'T MOVE!!" A dozen agents yelled as they ripped down the whole shower curtain, and dragged both Capo and Honey Bunz out of the shower butt naked and tossed them on the floor.

"Fuck is all this about?" Capo huffed as he Honey Bunz both were being hand cuffed.

"This is what this is all about" one agent said holding the book bag that Money Mike had given Honey Bunz the other night, while another agent placed the 9mm that laid on top of the toilet seat in a zip lock bag.

"We've been following you around all day," one of the agents said with a broad smile on his face.

"Fuck y'all crackers!" Capo huffed as he watched them destroy Honey Bunz's nice home looking for evidence. Capo grew even madder when he saw how the agents were looking at Honey Bunz bare-naked ass.

"Can I please put some clothes on?" Honey Bunz asked.

"Shut the fuck up and wait for my men to finish doing their job!" One of the agents said in a nasty tone still eyeing Honey Bunz's sexy body.

"Fuck!" Capo cursed. He knew he had fucked up and wouldn't be getting out of jail any time soon. Had Capo been on point, he definitely would have gone out in a blaze of glory.

"Sorry," Honey Bunz mouthed as they lifted her up and allowed her to put on a pair of sweat pants, and a white tee. Capo watched as all the agents laughed and smiled, making pervert remarks as they watched Honey Bunz get dress. The part that really killed him was that all he could do was watch the disrespect. Once Honey Bunz was escorted out of the house, the agents then lifted him up off the floor and allowed him to put his clothes back on.

# SILK WHITE

"I think this is the happiest day of my life," one of the agents said looking at Capo with a smile on his face. Capo thought about replying, but decided to hold his tongue. Nothing good would come from him opening his mouth. When the agents took Capo outside, he saw Honey Bunz mouth the words, "I love you," as the car she was in pulled off. Capo replied with a simple head nod as he lowered his head as he was placed in the back seat.

\*\*\*

Scarface and Shekia laughed all the way from the precinct, as they sat in the back seat cuddled up, while one of Scarface's goons drove.

"Bitch ass cops," Scarface chuckled as he turned to face Shekia. "Okay I need an answer from you."

"An answer?" Shekia repeated. She knew exactly what Scarface was talking about, but she hadn't really made up her mind yet.

"What you gon do?" Scarface asked in a serious tone. "I want you to be the queen to my castle."

"A move like this is crazy," Shekia admitted. "I mean I don't know nobody out here, no family, or nothing."

"I'm all the family you going to ever need," Scarface told her. "Besides you can always go back and visit your friends and family anytime you want." Shekia didn't say another word for the next four minutes.

"Okay"

"Okay what?" Scarface asked.

"Okay I'll come out here with you," Shekia told him. "I swear if you try to play me I'mma kill you," she threatened as the two kissed passionately as Scarface carried her from the car to the front door.

Shekia stepped foot in her new home, and could do nothing but smile from ear to ear. Before she could take another step in her new home, she heard her cell phone ringing. Shekia looked down at the screen and saw Kim's name flashing across it. "What the fuck she want?" Shekia thought as she answered. "Hello?"

"Yo, where you at?" Kim asked in a high pitch rushed voice. "I been trying to call you all night."

"I got caught up in a little something," Shekia replied. "Why, what's up?"

"Capo got locked up last night," Kim told her. "They are charging him with two counts of attempted murder, and some drugs, and weapon charges." From listening to Kim's voice on the other line Shekia could tell that Kim had been crying probably all night.

"Damn what his bail looking like?"

"They didn't give him one," Kim replied. "But fuck that I need you to come back and bring me that last package so I can make some moves."

"I got you," Shekia replied. "I'm about to get that and be on my way."

"Thank you so much I appreciate it, you like the only person I can trust right now," Kim said with desperation all in her voice. This was the first time Shekia could even remember having a real conversation with Kim. Shekia didn't want to leave Scarface, but she had one last job to do and then she was out. "Okay girl I'll call you when I touchdown," Shekia said flipping her phone closed.

"What's wrong?" Scarface asked as soon as Shekia closed her phone shut. Just from the look on her face he knew the news he was about to receive wasn't going to be good.

"Capo got locked up," Shekia began. "Kim just called me and said she needs me to drop off that last package."

"Right now?" Scarface asked with an attitude. She had just gotten there and he wasn't ready for her to leave just yet.

"This is my last drop off and I'm all done with this business," Shekia said.

"Plus, Capo has always looked out for me. I owe him this one last trip."

"You don't owe him shit!" Scarface cursed. He had heard about all the drama that had been popping off out in New York, and he heard about all the heat that was on Capo and his crew. Scarface pulled out his cell phone and dialed a number. "Set up the car for me and have it delivered to my house," he said into the phone before hanging it up.

***

Angela stepped foot inside her and James' home with a smile on her face. Today was the day that James was being released from the hospital, and she was too excited. Angela quickly went inside the kitchen, and started preparing dinner. She had the perfect night all planned out, just as Angela began to prepare the food, she heard somebody knocking on the front door. Instantly her hand removed the silenced .380 from her holster as she made her way to the door. She looked through the peephole and quickly put away her gun as she opened the door. Mr. Goldberg stood on the other side of the door.

"May I come in?"

"Sure," Angela said stepping to the side so the lawyer could come inside.

"Sorry to just pop up at your home like this but I have a very urgent message to give to you," Mr. Goldberg told her.

"So what's up?" Angela asked ready for some answers.

"Mr. Biggz is highly upset that you didn't finish the job you started with James Carter, but he became even more furious when he found out that you and James had been in a relationship," Mr. Goldberg told her.

"He feels as if you have betrayed him, and turned your back to him for a man. I spoke to him for about an hour and all he was talking about was how he couldn't believe that his number 2 would do him like that."

"So what did you come here for?" Angela said cutting straight to the chase. She knew Mr. Goldberg didn't come all the way to her house just to tell her that.

"The White Shadow is on his way to America," Mr. Goldberg said as his eyes dropped down to the floor. The only reason he was giving Angela the heads up was because he really liked and cared for her. The White Shadow was a Russian assassin, the number 1 and best assassin in the world. When Angela heard the name, she knew exactly whom Mr. Goldberg was talking about.

"Thanks for the heads up," Angela said with a nervous and worried look on her face. After all the years that Mr. Goldberg had known Angela, he had never seen her look as nervous as she did right now.

# SILK WHITE

"I don't know how much time you have," Mr. Goldberg said. "Just please take care of yourself and be careful," he said as he turned and left.

"Thanks," Angela yelled out as she closed and locked every lock on the door. Immediately, Angela ran upstairs, and transformed into her all-black outfit. She removed the big chest from the top of the closet and sat it on the bed, when she popped it open, all of her weapons looked up at her. The first thing Angela did was put on her custom-made Teflon vest. She then grabbed as many weapons as she could. Angela walked over to the mirror and looked at her reflection. A single tear ran down her face as she placed her black skullcap over her head. At that very moment, Angela knew that she had to leave town and do it fast if she wanted to live. She quickly packed as many of her and James's things as she could. "Fuck it, I'm just going to have to tell James the truth when he comes home," Angela said to herself as she sat the suitcase down right next to the door, then looked down at her watch.

\*\*\*

When Shekia finally made it back to New York, she badly needed to get some rest. All she wanted to do was give Kim the package and go on about her business. Shekia sang along with Erykah Badu as she pulled out her cell phone and dialed Kim's number. It rung several times then went straight to the voicemail. "Fuck!" Shekia sucked her teeth. Not knowing what else to do, she opened her phone back up and dialed Bone's number. He finally answered on the fourth ring. "Yo who dis?"

"It's Shekia, I got this package what you want me to do with it, I just called Kim, but she ain't answering."

"A'ight, bring that joint over to me," Bone said a little too eagerly. "I'm over here at the old spot."

"On my way," Shekia said snapping her phone shut. "I'm so glad I don't have to do this shit no more," she said out loud. Fifteen minutes later, Shekia pulled up to the old spot and saw Bone and about fifteen other men standing out front. "Hey Bone wassup?" Shekia asked in a friendly voice.

"You got the stuff?" Bone said looking at Shekia as if she was a total stranger.

"Yeah fool it's in the bumpers," Shekia said noticing the fresh bruise that Bone sported under his eye, along with a few other scratches. "What happened to your face?"

"Got fucked up by the cops," Bone lied as his goons began stripping the car right then and there.

"You got locked up with Capo?" Shekia asked.

"Huh Capo locked up?" Bone asked turning to face Shekia.

"Yeah he got locked up the other night," she told him. "I'm hearing he might to do some serious time too," Shekia said as she answered her ringing phone. "Hello?"

"Where you at?" Kim asked turning down the music in her car so she could hear.

"I'm here at the spot with Bone," Shekia said.

"What?" Kim yelled. "Please tell me you didn't give him the package!"

"Yeah why? I thought we were all on the same team?" Shekia said confused.

"Listen! Get out of there right now!" Kim told her. "Just run Bone is not on our team anymore." Just as Shekia turned around Bone, hit her across the face with his gun knocking her out instantly. He then picked up her cell phone and hung it up.

Once the phone went dead in Kim's ear, she immediately stomped on the gas heading to the spot. "Fuck!" she cursed knowing that Shekia was in trouble. Ten minutes later, Kim pulled up to the spot and saw Shekia laid out on the ground bleeding lying next to a stripped car.

"Oh my God," Kim said as she rushed out the car and ran to Shekia's aid. Once she saw how bad of condition Shekia was in, she immediately called 911.

# EPILOGUE

Once James was fully dressed, a smile quickly appeared on his face, he couldn't wait to go home to his baby. Angela had been by his bedside for the entire time he was injured and now he couldn't wait to get home to her.

"Hey Carter, you need to get over here and see this," one of his partners called out to him. James walked over and couldn't believe his eyes. On his partners laptop was a picture of the gunwoman with her sunglasses, hat and wig removed. The woman who James saw was his sweet lovely girlfriend Angela. Immediately, James felt betrayed, and then suddenly remembered that Angela told him that her parents were dead.

"Are you alright boss?"

"Yes I'm fine," James said with a sad but crazy look on his face. "Round up the boys, and lets go take this bitch down," James said as he and his crew strapped up and headed to his own house.

Angela paced back and forth waiting for James to arrive home. When she saw headlights beaming through the front window, she knew it James. Five minutes later, James walked through the front door with a bulletproof vest on with the letters F.B.I across the front, along with his .45 on his hip. Immediately, Angela knew something was up because he never wore his weapon while in the house.

"Hey baby is everything alright?" Angela said noticing a funny look on James face.

"Why wouldn't everything be alright?" James asked as he saw the suitcase resting by the door. "You going somewhere?"

# SILK WHITE

"Yes baby we have to leave town immediately, I'll tell you all about it on the way to the airport," Angela said moving in for a hug. James quickly took a step back and drew his .45 on her. "Don't fucking move!" He yelled. "Put them hands up!"

"Baby please we have to leave we don't have much time." Angela pleaded as she threw her hands up in surrender.

"The only place you're going is to jail," James said. "What you thought I wouldn't figure out who you really were?"

"Baby you know who I really am," Angel said hoping he would look past what she did for a living.

"Yeah I do know who you really are the Teflon Queen!" James said with a firm two-handed grip on his .45.

"Baby," Angela began as tears ran down her face. "I never meant to hurt you baby, but I'm in big trouble and we have to leave right now or else we're both going to die right here in this living room."

"Fuck you!" James growled. "Put your hands on the top of your head and turn around…. NOW!"

Angel did as she was told and slowly turned around as she watched James' every move from the reflection from the T.V. that was turned off. Once he got close enough, she quickly spun around, grabbed the nose of his gun, twisted James' wrist in an awkward direction causing him to drop the gun. "On the floor, now!" Angela yelled as she watched as James slowly dropped down to his knees. "If you don't want to come with me fine, but I have to go," just as those words left her mouth the front door came crashing down as several F.B.I agents filled the house wearing S.W.A.T team, and riot gear. "Drop your weapon and get on the ground now!" They ordered. Angela quickly stuck the .45 to James's forehead as she forcefully snatched him up to his feet and spun him around in a chokehold pressing the gun into James' temple. "Baby I will never hurt you," she whispered in James's ear as she quickly tried to come up with her next plan. As Angela looked at the F.B.I moving in on her, she saw a white man with a long blonde ponytail quietly enter through the front door. He wore an all-black suite with black leather gloves on each hand and moved as quiet as a cat. He held an M5 machine gun.

"Behind y'all!" James yelled out. When his team turned around the White Shadow was already in motion. He squeezed the trigger and waved his arms back and forth until every agent was laid out. Immediately, Angel took James down to the floor as she ran and fired the .45 at the ponytailed gunman. Once the White Shadow saw his target make a run for it, he squeezed the trigger again waving the gun at Angela and directed his aim in her path. Angela fired two more rounds. As she did, an army roll behind the counter in the kitchen. James quickly took cover behind the couch as he removed his spare 9mm. Angela placed her back up against the counter as she and James looked at one another. James gave her a head nod, which told her that for right now he was on her side. Angela tossed the .45 to the floor as she removed her silenced .380 from its holster. She then removed a small mirror from her back pocket. She stuck her arm around the corner with the mirror in her hand as she tried to locate the ponytailed gunman who could only be The White Shadow. Angela moved the mirror around but didn't see the gunman nowhere in sight. Seconds later, a bullet shot the mirror right out of Angela's hand.

The White Shadow removed a gas mask from the small of his back and placed it over his face. He grabbed four cans of sleeping gas. He pulled the pins from the sleeping gas and tossed two cans over the counter at Angela, and two over the couch at James.

"Fuck!" Angela cursed as she snatched the skully off her head. She flicked her wrist, and the knife sat right in the palm of her hand. She quickly cut up the hat and then placed it around her mouth and nose so the gas wouldn't affect her. Angela looked over at James who was now knocked out from the gas. On the silent count of three, Angela sprung up

# SILK WHITE

from behind the counter with a two handed grip on her .380 she looked through the entire living room and didn't see anybody. She slowly inched her way through the living room, squinting her eyes in search of the ponytailed gunman. Out the blue, Angela saw a leg come out of nowhere and kicked the gun out of her hand. The same leg then kicked her in the face, causing her to stumble backwards. Standing in front of Angela was the White Shadow. Immediately, Angel threw a quick jab followed by a hook. The White Shadow blocked the first jab, and weaved the hook as he landed a straight open hand to Angela's face. He threw a quick sidekick at Angela, she weaved it by inches as she caught his leg, and foot swept him dropping him down on his back. The White Shadow quickly lifted his other leg and kicked Angela across the face. The White Shadow laid on his back and pulled a 9mm from his holster.

Angela quickly turned and tried to make a run for it. As she ran, she removed her other .380 jumping through the front window, as two bullets exploded in her back and side forcing her completely out the window. Angela landed on her side on the front lawn. The first thing she did was return fire. Even though Angela was in pain, she knew she had to get out of there. It took all her strength to get back up as she limped to her Red Lamborghini. She hopped in the front seat and backed out of the driveway. The White Shadow hopped out the front window with his M5 in his hand. He squeezed the trigger waving his arms back and forth. Angela placed the Lambo in drive and peeled off as she heard bullets pinging and bouncing off her car.

The White Shadow quickly jogged over to his all-black Aston Martin. He hopped behind the wheel and gunned the engine. He kept one eye on the road as he reloaded his 9mm with the extended clip doing about 90 miles per hour.

"What the fuck!" Angela yelled as she touched her side while she flew down the street. She was happy that the bullet didn't rip through her vest. She kept peeking through the rear view mirror as she maneuvered from lane to lane at a high speed.

# THE TEFLON QUEEN

The White Shadow stuck his arm out the window and fired two shots at the Lamborghini's back window. Angela ducked down as she heard her back window shatter. She quickly made a fishtailed turn on to the highway as she flew down the ramp. "Think, think, think," Angela yelled as she banged on the steering wheel.

The White Shadow stuck his arm out the window and fired three shots at Angela's back tire.

Angela gripped the steering wheel as she lost control of the car. The Lamborghini spun around about three to four times before two other cars crashed into her causing her car to finally come to a stop. Angela felt the warm blood trickling down her face as she looked up, and saw the White Shadow slowly getting out his car with a gun in his hand. Angela panicked as she searched around the car for her .380 she had dropped it during the crash. She felt down on the floor searching for it as she saw the White Shadow getting closer and closer...........

## To Be Continued...

# ACKNOWLEDGEMENT

Thanks to all of my fans for riding with me...
Hope you enjoyed!

# SILK WHITE

## Books by Good2Go Authors

# SILK WHITE

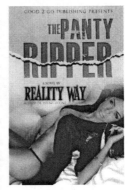

## Good2Go Films Presents

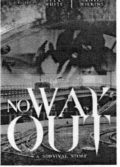

# THE TEFLON QUEEN

*To order books, please fill out the order form below:*
*To order films please go to* www.good2gofilms.com

Name: _____

Address: _____

City: _____ State: _____ Zip Code: _____

Phone: _____

Email: _____

Method of Payment:  ☐ Check   ☐ VISA   ☐ MASTERCARD

Credit Card#: _____

Name as it appears on card: _____

Signature: _____

| Item Name | Price | Qty | Amount |
|---|---|---|---|
| 48 Hours to Die – Silk White | $14.99 | | |
| He Loves Me, He Loves You Not - Mychea | $14.99 | | |
| He Loves Me, He Loves You Not 2 - Mychea | $14.99 | | |
| He Loves Me, He Loves You Not 3 - Mychea | $14.99 | | |
| Married To Da Streets – Silk White | $14.99 | | |
| My Boyfriend's Wife - Mychea | $14.99 | | |
| Never Be The Same – Silk White | $14.99 | | |
| Stranded – Silk White | $14.99 | | |
| Slumped – Jason Brent | $14.99 | | |
| Tears of a Hustler - Silk White | $14.99 | | |
| Tears of a Hustler 2 - Silk White | $14.99 | | |
| Tears of a Hustler 3 - Silk White | $14.99 | | |
| Tears of a Hustler 4- Silk White | $14.99 | | |
| Tears of a Hustler 5 – Silk White | $14.99 | | |
| Tears of a Hustler 6 – Silk White | $14.99 | | |
| The Panty Ripper - Reality Way | $14.99 | | |
| The Teflon Queen – Silk White | $14.99 | | |
| The Teflon Queen 2 – Silk White | $14.99 | | |
| The Teflon Queen – 3 – Silk White | $14.99 | | |
| The Teflon Queen 4 – Silk White | $14.99 | | |
| Time Is Money - Silk White | $14.99 | | |
| Young Goonz – Reality Way | $14.99 | | |
| | | | |
| Subtotal: | | | |
| Tax: | | | |
| Shipping (Free) U.S. Media Mail: | | | |
| Total: | | | |

**Make Checks Payable To:  Good2Go Publishing - 7311 W Glass Lane, Laveen, AZ 85339**